OF CURSES AND CHARMS

SISTER WITCHES OF RAVEN FALLS COZY
MYSTERY SERIES, BOOK 2

NYX HALLIWELL

Beach
Path
Publishing
LLC

Of Curses and Charms

Sister Witches of Raven Falls Cozy Mystery Series, Book 2

© 2019 Nyx Halliwell

ISBN: 978-1-948686-14-3

Print ISBN: 978-1-948686-29-7

Cover Art by EDH Graphics

Formatting by Beach Path Publishing, LLC

Editing by Elizabeth Neal, Cheryl Giebel

Please Note

ACKNOWLEDGMENTS

Long-life and fair health to all who've worked to bring this book into the world. My amazing family, sweet friends, editors (couldn't do without you, Beth and Cheryl), beta readers (Amy, as always, you're the best), and my street team who leave the BEST reviews.

Blessed be,
    Nyx and the sisters

WITCHES' CREED

Thirteen powers do the Witches claim
their right of lineage by the Goddess's name.
Tie a knot and say the words
or hand on head – the blessing conferred.
A Witch can give success in love
curse or bless through God/dess above.
Speak to beasts and spirits alike
command the weather, cast out a blight.
Read the heavens and stars of the night
divine the future and give good advice.
Conjure treasure and bring fortune to bear
heal the sick and kill despair.
This is my birthright to have and share
blessings you, dear reader, may the spirits be fair.

1

I have a confession... I can see the future.

That is, for everyone except my sisters. The three people in this world I want to protect most.

I'm Summer Whitethorne, fire witch. My favorite time of the year, the Summer Solstice, is only a few days away, falling on my birthday this year. The one wish—the *only* wish—I have is to see what's going to happen to the four of us.

I touch my mother's crystal wand, lying on my dresser, and it instantly reveals a secret she tried to keep from us before she died. One I have yet to tell Spring, Autumn, and Winter.

Along with the gift of claircognizance, I have the Touch. Psychometry is the one thing I wish I didn't possess as I often pick up messages I'd rather not when I touch people or things. Mostly it happens when death is near, and combined with my ability to see the future, it creates quite a conundrum for me. I detest lies and secrets, but I can't go around telling people when and how they're going to die.

Harm none...the spirit of that rule is one I embrace

whenever possible. Foretelling someone's future can certainly create more harm than good.

Leaving my cabin with a fresh pair of fingerless lace gloves, I step outside and warm summer air flows over me. It's Monday and my to-do list is as long as my broomstick. While I'd love to skinny dip in the hot spring or go hunting for crystals in the cave next to it, I'm looking forward to marking everything off my list during these longest of days.

Cinders, my familiar, calls a good morning as he flies down to land on his perch. The Phoenix is a mythological creature, but after a near-death experience at four years old, I conjured one for myself.

Mother had read me a bedtime story about a beautiful witch transforming into a phoenix upon her death in a fire set by her enemies. Not exactly your normal bedtime story at that age, but I wasn't exactly normal. The fictional witch rose from the ashes in order to protect her family, and it's still my favorite story. When I accidently drowned in the hot spring at four, it was Cinders I met on the other side of the veil who brought me back to life.

Since he bursts into flames at inconvenient times, he stays outside and rarely goes close to the woods. This morning, I greet him with a stroke of his feathers and a handful of shredded carrots for his breakfast.

"We have a lot to do," I tell him, my jet and carnelian bracelets making a soft clicking noise on my wrist as I pet him. "I hope you're ready."

He squawks and rustles his wings, the red and blue feathers soft and new, telling me we should be safe from a fiery transformation until the full moon. That's his normal time for going up in flames, but if he becomes alarmed or stressed, he erupts early.

As he gulps his food, I make an offering to my goddess,

Hestia, protector of hearth and flame. "North, South, East, and West, protection and health as you know best. This is my will, so shall it be. Thank you, goddess. Blessed be."

I set off toward Conjure, the shop my sisters and I own. We sell a variety of products and services for those into holistic, organic, and Wiccan living and carry everything from baked goods and jewelry to bath products and home décor. My love is crystals, and I have a section devoted strictly to them, including raw and tumbled stones, wands, and assorted jewelry.

People think witches sacrifice animals, worship Satan, or put curses on them. In reality, the majority of us drink a lot of tea, have too many cats, are into crystals and smudging, and mostly want to be left alone.

The temperature is climbing into the eighties, but there's little humidity and I enjoy the sun on my face and smelling the flowers and herbs my sister, Spring, has planted along the path. The lavender is blooming, filling the air with the sweet scent along with roses and hydrangeas. A smattering of wild violets are interspersed with the other plants, and I stop and pick a few to weave into my braid.

The shop doesn't open until nine, but the kitchen light is on and Spring is inside. As I get closer, a breeze passes over me and I smell warm sugar and vanilla. She's baking and my gift shows me a pie in the oven. I see a bit of the purple juice bubbling from the browning crust and know it's made with the berries we gathered in the forest yesterday. I'm hoping for a blueberry cake for my birthday, too.

Looks like I'm having pie for breakfast.

Cinders flies by overhead. "Pie for breakfast?"

At least that's what his squawk says to me. Another thing that came out of my near-death experience—I can hear certain animals talking as if they're human. Normal people hear barks, growls, chirping, etc., but my brain translates it into messages I understand. Not all species, but certain ones, like Cinders, tell me quite a few things.

"Hey, it's fruit, all right?" I retort. "It's no worse than one of Spring's muffins or scones."

He makes another squawk and it sounds like laughter.

I'm nearly to the back porch when Godfrey, Conjure's resident cat, shoots around the corner. The beautiful black cat looks alarmed, which puts me on alert.

Godfrey doesn't react that way to *anything*, unless it's his empty food dish, which being the diva he is, resides on a special antique dresser in the shop. He refuses to eat on the floor. Godfrey only has two modes—cat napping and eating.

"Small beasts! Extreme noise!" he yells in my head, a high pitch screeching noise coming from his physical mouth. He's named for the great inventor because he insists he's the genius reincarnated.

"Small beasts?"

"Make it stop!" he yells at me. My sisters often understand him too, since he was our mother's familiar and has a special bond with all of us. Unfortunately, we're regularly subjected to his demands, including the fact he insists we should call him God and leave the "frey" off, since he's superior to us and is full of disdain for us regular humans. He constantly plies me with formulas and equations that mean absolutely nothing to me.

"What kind?" I ask.

"Wiggly ones!" he shouts.

That casual word is not in his normal lexicon. He's really shaken up. "Could you be more specific? Where are they?"

He flicks his tail, a slight curl on the end, before turning on his forepaws and leading me around the outside of the shop.

4

"I don't have time for distractions today, Godfrey," I tell him, wondering how far we're going and why he's so upset.

He takes me to the front porch, the closed sign still in view since it's an hour before opening and marches up the steps.

On the porch, all I see is a ragged cardboard box, the flaps folded in on themselves. On the side in slanted writing are the words *Please Help* in black marker.

As I jog up the steps, a tiny cry goes up, a tiny sound that goes straight to my heart.

Dropping to my knees, I reach for the box as Godfrey hops up on the small round table off to the side with two chairs for visitors to sit and chat. On the heels of the first small cry, another joins in followed by a third.

I don't need claircognizance to know what's inside.

Peeling back the flaps, my heart does a little skip. Inside are nestled five tiny kittens, not more than two weeks old, their eyes still closed.

Tiny paws reach toward each other as they fumble over themselves and the blanket someone left with them.

I glance around the parking lot and across the street to the woods, but there's no sign of who put them here. They're so young that without their mother their odds of survival are slim.

The mewing grows louder, shriller, as they sense I'm near. From the north, I hear a familiar vehicle approaching, and a moment later, our neighbor Hopper Caldwell pulls in.

I reach in and pet each in turn, cooing and trying to reassure them they'll be okay. Mentally, I send questions but get nothing back. They have no idea who their mother is, what happened to her, or how they ended up here.

The little bodies are cool to the touch where they should be warm, especially in this heat. I'm already starting to sweat a little along my hairline. It's definitely going to be a blistering warm June day.

I need to get them inside, figure out what to feed them. Hopefully, Spring will have the recipe for Mom's special formula.

"Good morning," Hopper calls as he bails out of his truck. In his hands, he carries three books and a velvet bag. He's pulled his mahogany colored hair away from his face in a tiny man-bun at the base of his neck, the sun picking up auburn highlights in it and his beard. His worn jeans and Metallica t-shirt belay the fact he's a millionaire. "Whatcha got there?"

My heart does a happy skip at his presence. "Someone dumped kittens on our porch. They're too young to be away from their mother."

His boots echo on the steps as he comes beside me, bending over to look. He smells good, like he recently got out of the shower.

He sets his things on the table and Godfrey makes a face and jumps down, jetting as far away as he can get.

Hopper's big hand is gentle as he strokes one of the kitten's heads. "We better get them inside," he says. He motions at me to take the books and bag before he lifts the box.

I always carry thin lace gloves to put on if I have to touch anything. Today it's a pair my mother made me. She was always knitting, crocheting, or weaving. Her loom and needles sit untouched in Winter's cabin.

Pulling them on, I unlock the door and he brings the kittens into the coolness of the shop. "Take them to my treatment room," I tell him.

Godfrey bangs through the cat door and hops on the

counter, keeping his eyes on the box. "Too much racket! Make it stop!"

They mewl loudly from the rough treatment, poor things, even though the giant man carrying them is doing so as gently and reverently as a mother would a sleeping baby.

"Hush," I murmur to Godfrey under my breath. "They'll die if we don't help them."

He raises his black nose and gives a little snort.

We're not allowed to have animals in the kitchen where Spring bakes, so I call to her as we pass the doorway "Spring, I need you."

Hopper uses his booted foot to push the door open to my tiny treatment room where I do crystal consultations and energy work. He sets the box on the table and once more begins petting the kittens, his low voice soothing as he speaks endearments.

The anxious mewing morphs into sounds of curiosity as they struggle to get into his hands. A couple try to suck on his fingers, while a white one with orange spots climbs up his arm.

Hopper laughs softly, a smile spreading across his bearded face. This side of him amazes me, even though I've seen it before. His appearance is that of a rough mountain man, or a biker from some motorcycle gang, so seeing the softer side of him is always a pleasant surprise.

He glances at me with that smile and my heart melts a little. "You can save them, right?"

I detach the white and orange kitten's nails from his arm and hold it close to my chest. Through the palm of my hands I feel its weak heartbeat as well as its determination to live.

I don't want to see the future because I know its chances

of survival are less than fifty percent, but it comes anyway. I smile at Hopper, camouflaging the dread I feel. "Of course."

Spring rushes in, her blonde hair in a ponytail, cheeks flushed from the heat in the kitchen. She's carrying a dishtowel, drying her hands on it. "What's wrong?" Her eyes go to the tiny being I'm holding, then to the box and Hopper. "Goddess above, where did those come from?"

I tell her about Godfrey leading me to them. "Someone abandoned them here."

She frowns. "What do you need me to do?"

"We need something for them to eat. We'll have to hand feed them, probably with droppers to start." *A little magick might be in order, too*, I offer telepathically.

A nod, determination like that of the small kitten flooding through her. "I have mom's formula recipe for abandoned baby animals. I used it on the squirrels I found this past spring in the forest, remember? I'll tweak it for these little guys. Be right back."

Hopper disengages his hands after a bit of struggle. One nearly made it all the way up to the Death Before Dishonor tattoo on his bicep, but he doesn't seem annoyed by the tiny nail pricks. "I have a heat lamp at my place. Do you want me to get it?"

His antique shop three miles north is where he lives, our closest neighbor, but still, the time it'll take to get there and back may be too much. These guys need to warm-up and eat now.

"Spring has grow-lamps in the greenhouse," I tell him. "There are three by three boxes for seedlings as well. They might be the perfect size. Can you grab one of each?"

He nods and takes off. "Don't worry," he calls over his shoulder. "It'll be okay."

Hopper knows I'm a witch, but I'm not sure what his

concept of that is. Many people have a basic concept of Wicca, but not true magick. Seeing it in action can scare them. He definitely doesn't know I can see the future or get hits off certain things I touch.

I've touched him.

I wish I hadn't.

My treatment table has a gemstone mat on it that heats, so I turn it on, clicking the infrared and photon options as well. The little guy I'm holding mews raggedly, but then I feel a soft vibration under my hands.

Purring.

Thank you, the teeny, tiny voice barely registers in my mind, but it's there. My mothering instincts kick in hard, and I close my eyes. Once again, the future flashes across my mind.

The kitten's chances are growing stronger.

2

*C*onfession number two—seeing the future is a curse.

People think if they know what lies ahead, life will be better, they'll be able to avoid tragedy, or keep their loved ones safe. Mostly, they're wrong. Free will is a valuable tool, but some things are determined by fate. Knowing what might happen only seems to create more chaos, confusion, and fear.

It's one of the reasons I've chosen to never have children. I don't want to pass this curse on to them. I suspect my mother had the Touch, although she never confided in me if she did.

For the next hour, Summer, Hopper, and I make sure the kittens are warm and fed. We use droppers to get formula into them and soon they fall to sleep.

"What are we going to name them?" Hopper asks.

Godfrey makes his presence known. "Chaos, Disaster, Havoc, Bedlam, Maelstrom, you get the idea." He jumps on the table and sniffs the air over the box.

Hush, I mentally tell him.

He meows indignantly. It sounds to me like he says, "I have more! Trouble, Inconvenience, Strife, Misery, Nuisance."

I shoo him away. Mom would never let us name any of the wild babies we took in and nurtured because they'd lost their mothers, before returning them to their natural habitat. Claiming if we did, we'd get too attached. I suppose that's true, but my sisters and I were instantly crazy about each that came along and secretly named all of them.

For a second, I hesitate to let Hopper believe they're going to make it because it's way too soon to tell for sure. But there's an energy behind attachment. Willing something to live can often provide the tipping point to give the small animal a little extra fight.

"Do you have any in mind?" I ask as he picks up the box to move it.

It's opening time and we put the kittens behind the cash register, placing them on a covered heating pad set on low. Hopper finagles the heat lamp to hang over them where they're nestled inside a sturdy wooden container. "I'm thinking," he says.

Spring added several blankets for them to nestle in, and I retrieve one of our popular teddy bear rice bags. They're great for children, scented with lavender, and easy to warm in the microwave. The rice will absorb the heat and give the kittens something to curl up next to, a surrogate mother.

Hopper sits on the floor behind the counter watching them. "They need big names to counterbalance how small they are."

Spring returns from the kitchen, bringing each of us a piece of her warm blackberry pie and a cup of coffee. I take a bite and a drink before I go to the door and unlock it, flipping the sign to announce we're open.

"I agree," Spring says to Hopper. "Since there are five, we should do a theme."

I down more of the pie and coffee. "What about famous landmarks?" One of my dreams is to travel to foreign places —which will probably never happen, since I have so much responsibility here.

The bell over the door jingles as our first customer arrives and the noise wakes one of the kittens. She mews plaintively.

Spring greets the customer, leaving me and Hopper to watch the babies. Two more begin crying as well, and he pets them gently. "This one's the color of whiskey," he says. "We could use different types of liquor."

The other three stir, adding to the chorus of cries. Hopper laughs softly as they all try to climb onto his hands.

Most of them sound like kittens to me, only the one I heard earlier occasionally communicating something more human sounding. He's the runt of the litter, but his cry is deep. They all have different vocal qualities reminding me of a human choir.

"What do you have back there?" The customer leans over the counter. She's a young woman with dark hair and even darker eyes. "Awe, they're so cute."

After another moment of admiring them, she returns to shopping and Spring joins us. "Boy, for little guys, they sure are loud," she says, laughing.

"Yes, they have their own symphony, don't they?" I ask.

Hopper snaps his fingers "That's it. Rock bands?" He points to his t-shirt.

Hmm. Not quite what I was thinking. "How about composers?" I offer. "Mozart. Bach, Chopin? Something classy, you know?"

He looks a little crestfallen and shrugs. "Okay, but don't forget Beethoven."

"Those are male names," Spring says. "Are the kittens all boys?"

"Two females." I've already checked. "How about Vivaldi for a girl?"

Hopper nods. "There are plenty of female composers."

I'm ashamed of the fact my sister and I look at him blankly.

"You know," he says "Clara Shuman? Fanny Mendelssohn?"

We both shake our heads. Some feminists we are.

"Surely you've heard of Hildegard of Bingen."

Shameful shakes again.

"Come on, St. Hildegard? Also known as Sybil of the Rhine? She's one of the earliest women composers on record. Lived in the twelfth century. She was a German Benedictine Abbess, a real badass." He ticks things off with this fingers. "A writer, philosopher, Christian mystic and visionary. She's considered the founder of scientific natural history in Germany."

At our blank looks he hangs his head. "I can't believe you ladies haven't heard of her."

"Wow," Spring says. "She sounds like a goddess. That's impressive."

It certainly is, but I can't imagine naming either of the females—both with dark gray stripes—Hildegard. "I do like Sybil."

Hopper scratches his whiskered jaw. "Hildegard is an awesome name. Kickass like you sisters."

The way it rolls off his tongue, I have to agree. Plus, I enjoy how he's smiling at me, his compliment. "St. Hildegard," I try it out. "Not bad."

Hopper pulls out the formula and dropper and begins feeding the kittens once more. "So, we have Beethoven, Mozart, Chopin, Vivaldi, and Hildegard. What an awesome bunch."

Our dark-haired customer returns with a bracelet, a can of loose tea, two bottles of essential oils, and incense. "If you need to find homes, let me know. I'd love to adopt one or two."

I see Hopper resisting the idea, and won't be surprised if he tries to take them all home.

She leaves, the kittens go back to sleep, and I finish my pie. Somehow when it's made from berries we picked ourselves, it always tastes better.

Hopper hands the books he brought to Spring. "Came across these at Mariel Fontaine's estate sale over the weekend," he tells her. "She had a huge library with quite a collection of antique and vintage editions. These have information on Raven Falls, and one is all about legends concerning this area. Summer told me you're interested in the history of your property, so I thought you might like them."

Spring and I exchange a glance. He has no idea why she's so interested in what's happened here through the centuries, and I don't plan to tell him. I can never leave our forty-four acres in the Pacific Northwest because my sisters and I are gatekeepers, ensuring an entity remains imprisoned in the earth here. The thing we call a demon killed our mother last fall on Samhain, and Spring encountered it again at Beltane. One of its minions referred to it as "the master."

Whatever it is, it's evil, and we're trying to find a way to destroy it. Unfortunately, so far, we haven't had any luck.

"That's awesome, Hopper," she says, accepting them. "Thank you."

Hopper grabs the bag next and hands it to me. "I bought a dozen or so boxes as well. A couple have vintage jewelry in them. This is one of the pieces. I thought you might like it because of the stones."

Inside is a Victorian style necklace in the shape of a snake. I hesitate to pull it out, afraid of the Touch kicking in but I can't exactly not examine it with him watching me.

I spread the cloth napkin Spring gave me earlier on the counter and gently tip the bag so the necklace falls onto it. I pull on my gloves and see the eyes are garnets.

"It's beautiful," I tell him. "You should really keep this in your store and sell it."

"I'd rather you have it. I'm not even sure the gemstones are real."

Garnets are much more than pretty, semi-precious stones. They've been used for protection, strength, and light since before the Bronze Age in all sorts of cultures.

Pharaohs had jewelry made from them, Christians used them as talismans. In my energy healing work, they help to strengthen the physical body and aid blood flow. Some days when I'm feeling tired or off balance, I carry a set of polygon garnets in my pockets or bra. They never fail to give me a boost and protect me from energy vampires.

Because I'm so familiar with them, I can recognize them and confirm they're real. "It's an amazing piece," I tell Hopper, "and these are definitely real."

"I want you to have the necklace," he says, and pats one of my hands. "Those stones are kind of fiery, aren't they? When I saw them, they reminded me of you."

Fire is my natural element. It's why I love this season so

much. Mother named me after the hottest days of the year, and fire is in my blood.

Hopper's touch makes that internal fire climb higher, and I'm mesmerized by his cool, gray eyes. In all honesty, he's perfect for me. Calm, steady, grounding.

With my element, I usually seek the air to feed it, so I need water and earth to balance me out. It's why Spring and I get along well—she's heavy on the earth element, yet has enough air in her birth chart to keep me burning.

Something passes between me and Hopper, like it often does when I stop long enough to really look at him. He's a gentle teddy bear inside the body of a gruff giant, and I wish with all of my heart our relationship could develop beyond friendship.

His touch becomes firmer, his fingers brushing mine, and I have to pull away. Not because I don't like it—I love it. But the lace gloves are fingerless and touch means pain if I get a hit about his future again.

He backs up and clears his throat, glances at the kittens as if nothing happened between us, but I feel his uncertainty now, his disappointment I didn't return his affection.

"Guess I better get back to my shop," he says. "Almost time for me to open, too."

"Thank you for everything." I follow him, guilty about my reaction and desperate to smooth things over. "I mean it. Your timing was perfect this morning."

Spring pretends to be busy cleaning the dishes and cups, giving us a sense of privacy. Hopper stops at the door and turns to me with a shy smile. "I can help more, if you need it, with the kittens. Just call if you guys get too busy, or have clients and can't watch them."

I risk laying a hand on his arm. I wish he was one of the people I couldn't read.

"I could use help this afternoon with a client, if you have time, Mrs. Sorensen's arthritis is too bad to drive, so she can't come here for her regular weekly treatment. I have an idea about how to help her, but I have to go to her."

This seems to cheer him up. "What time do you want me here?"

"Two o'clock?"

He gives me a roguish smile before opening the door. "See you then, Summer."

After he leaves Spring says, "What kind of treatment?"

"I'm going to haul spring water to her."

"The hot spring helps her joints, doesn't it?"

"Yes, she's been soaking in it once a week for the past month. Between that and our energy sessions, we were seeing real progress. She skipped last week because one of her daughters was in town. Now she's so stiff, and her joints are in so much pain, she can't drive. I'm not sure why her caretaker can't bring her, but it doesn't matter. I don't mind going to her house."

"It's going to take a lot of water, isn't it?"

"That's why I need help. I'll fill up her bathtub, use magick to heat it, and put her in it."

"I'll babysit the kittens while you're gone." She disappears into the kitchen.

I check on the small bodies and see they're still sleeping. The necklace lies on the countertop and I sincerely wish I could wear it.

Sometimes I can clear the energies lodged in an object, but it usually takes some doing. I'm not sure it will be a problem, but I go to my treatment room cabinet and pull out a large glass bowl and a bag of Himalayan salt.

Back at the counter, I pour salt into the bowl and use a pencil to pick up the necklace and drop it in. With the pencil eraser, I push the necklace under the tiny pink chunks.

For the next several hours, I work on the Conjure blog, upload an informational video on citrine to our YouTube channel, rearrange a display of crystal wands, and take care of the kittens, holding and feeding them each time they wake.

Autumn arrives at noon for a client consultation, and Winter drags herself in shortly after that. Both of my older sisters immediately fall in love with the kittens and offer their help.

Winter doesn't like to run the shop, but she agrees to take over while I help Mrs. Sorensen. Spring brings me the latest recipe to put on the blog for tomorrow and I get that scheduled.

I move the bowl off to the side and plan to leave it overnight before saging it to clear the previous owner's energy.

As it nears two, I try to slide past Winter. She's leaning over the makeshift kitten incubator. My skirt catches on a hook we hang keys on and Godfrey darts across my feet. In an attempt not to step on him, I bump into her.

Balance...one thing I lack.

She tries to catch me as I tip sideways, but in an effort to keep us both from going over, I reach out to grab the counter. My hand sends the bowl flying in the air.

Salt spills. Instinctively, I throw both hands out to try and catch it, and hear the bell over the door at the same instant. Hopper's smiling face comes into view as salt flows over my hands and the bowl crashes into the stool behind the cash register.

Godfrey hollers and jets off.

Winter has better luck, but I end up with the necklace

on the tips of my fingers as I crash to the floor. My fingers close over it and I latch onto the silver.

The room spins. In the blink of an eye, I'm no longer in the shop.

The house smells like old people, filled with Victorian furniture and oil portraits on the walls. There seems to be a party going on and people laughing and drinking, talking and dancing in a large room.

"What do you think, my dear?" A man asks. He holds out a velvet box. "Do you like it?"

He opens it. I gasp and reach for the necklace inside—the silver snake. The hands I see are not mine, they are much more elegant, and one has a beautiful garnet ring on it. I don't know what's happening, but I hear myself say, "I love it. It's beautiful."

The man moves to clasp it around my neck. "Happy birthday, darling."

I feel a rush of love for him.

The Touch is showing me the last owner receiving the piece as a gift. I'm feeling what she felt, seeing what she saw.

And then, with it around my neck, my stomach cramps, my head spins. I feel lightheaded and dizzy. "I must sit down," I tell the man.

Strong hands grip my arms. "What's wrong?"

I see him again—his moustache and beard, his very serious eyes searching mine. He helps me to a red velvet chair.

"I'm not sure," I say, my voice breathy. There's a metallic taste in my mouth, a buzz of something familiar around my heart. It's magick, but none like I've felt before. "Perhaps I should go upstairs and lie—"

Everything goes dark.

3

$\mathcal{I}$ wake to find Hopper's handsome face hovering above me. His lips move, but my ears pop like I'm underwater and I can't understand what he's saying.

Everything inside my body aches, my hand spasms, clenching and releasing over and over again. I feel sick, although the sensation is waning. I have to keep blinking to focus, concentrating on the deep lines in Hopper's forehead as a focal point.

Someone touches the top of my head lightly and I'm instantly filled with magickal energy. It's refreshing, like Spring because my sister is sending healing energy to help me recover.

As the underwater sensation seeps away, I begin to hear a variety of sounds—mewing kittens, the ringing phone, the soft spell Spring is speaking over me. Hopper's questions.

"Summer, can you hear me? Are you okay? Talk to me."

Things fade in and out like a radio station that can't quite lock on the right frequency. I swallow past the dryness in my throat, allowing Spring's magick to calm my stomach the rest of the way and reboot my system.

Godfrey is behind Hopper, cleaning his fur with great nonchalance. *Puuhlease, she's fine,* I hear him say. *I'm the one who nearly got trampled on!*

"I'm okay," I tell her, which sounds ridiculous even to me, since I'm lying on the ground, knocked unconscious by a cat and a necklace.

The vision of the woman swims in my brain, like a dream I can't quite hang on to. I raise my hands so Hopper and Spring stop talking, but the phone keeps ringing and the kitties keep crying. My head throbs hard, as if it might burst.

I desperately need to hold onto the last tendril of memory, that connection to the woman who wore the necklace. For some reason it consumes me. Like a spinning wheel, I reel the memory back in, anchoring it in my brain, feeling it in my breastbone. I'm not sure why—there's something she suspected that cowers in the back of my memory. I have to know what it is.

I don't want to lose this, so I make myself return to what I saw, felt, heard around me. I log each detail, creating a spell that'll help me recall it later.

When I finally nod, Spring and Hopper help me sit. He raises three fingers in front of my eyes. "How many am I holding up?"

He's so endearing, for a moment all I can do is chuckle. "You're holding up fingers?" I tease.

It's a bad joke. He thinks I'm serious. "We need to get her to the hospital. You hit your head pretty hard," he says to me. "You must have a concussion." He calls over his shoulder. "Can somebody get an ice bag?"

The back of my head does hurt, and some ice would be good, but the pain is melting away, thanks to Spring's spell. "I'm okay," I stress again. "Just let me sit a minute."

Spring kneels beside my legs. "What happened?"

"The Touch." She'll know what that means.

Hopper holds my shoulder as I lean against the side of the counter. "What's that?"

I glance to my left, still feeling the energy from the necklace lying on the floor, abandoned. The phone has stopped, thanks to Winter, but the kittens are still agitated and my ears are insanely sensitive. I feel their cries all the way to my bones. Salt spilled around us and I realize the necklace will need a lot more cleaning than I suspected. The woman's spirit is strongly attached to it.

I meet Hopper's worried gaze, knowing if I tell him, he might decide I'm too weird for his comfort zone.

Maybe that'd be a good thing. I can never have a lasting relationship with anyone, especially not if they want a family.

My heart beats hard, fear of losing him flooding my system. I can almost see the future. Sadness will swamp me if he gets that look in his eyes that says I'm crazy and he needs to get away from me.

This is Hopper, I tell myself. *He would never walk out on you. He would never look at you that way. He knows you're a witch and he still comes to see you every day.*

He's reading my hesitancy, and he puts his other hand on my knee and leans toward me slightly. "It's okay, Summer. I know you have secrets. I do, too. You don't have to tell me if you don't want to."

By the goddess, how did I get so lucky? "I could use a cup of tea, Spring," I say. "Hopper can you help me to the kitchen?"

Autumn rushes in as Hopper is helping me to my feet. Winter's still on the phone. "I got here as fast as I could." She looks me over. "What happened?"

"Lost my balance, hit my head." Mentally, I send her the rest of the explanation. She glances between me and Hopper and nods.

"Can you watch the store a moment," Spring asks. "I'll be right back to clean up the salt."

A customer comes in and Autumn greets her. Hopper gently guides me to the back, where I sit while Spring puts water onto boil and picks out tea. Hopper disappears and a moment later, he comes back with the kittens.

"We can't have animals in here," Spring says. "The health department could shut me down."

Hopper glances around and gives an exaggerated shrug. "I don't see anyone here from the health department, do you, Summer?"

He grins and Spring rolls her eyes, caving far too easily.

That's an impressive feat—Spring is obsessive about keeping her kitchen clean and free of pet hair. Godfrey appears in the door, acting as if he's going to walk right in.

Sensing him, Spring whirls and pins him with a look. I hear her warn him she'll singe his fur if he tries it. With a haughty look, he strolls on by.

As if he's an old pro at it now, Hopper retrieves formula from the refrigerator and warms it in a pan on the stove. While they're both busy, I concentrate on what I'm going to tell him.

The truth would be best, and it seems like the right thing to do. He's a good man, and I want to be honest, especially if we're going to have any kind of relationship, even just as friends.

I dated a lot in high school but was never serious about anyone. I didn't go to college, and most of the guys in Raven Falls aren't open to magick. There are a few who practice natural living and embrace energy work, but actual magick and witchcraft? No way.

Spring is luckier. She's found a partner who has magick himself and can understand our world, even though he's the chief of police. Tristan MacGregor is also a good guy, like Hopper, but he was forced to accept his own abilities. He had no choice. Hopper, on the other hand, is just a muggle. Not a drop of magick in him that I can sense.

Spring sets out my favorite teapot, the one with the large honeybee on it. She pours tea for us, and I smell ginger— good for settling the stomach. She must've picked up on my nausea when she was sending magick into me.

She also gets out a plate of her newest creation— crackers made from quinoa, seeds and nuts. I thank her as Hopper tests the formula and decides it's the perfect temperature.

He sets their box on a chair in a sunny spot and begins feeding them as Spring heads out once more.

He picks up Mozart and coaxes the small kitten to suck on the end of the dropper. "You're sure you're okay?" Concern still creases his forehead.

I sip the warm tea, feeling it go all the way to my belly. "I will be. This isn't the first time I've had one of these spells."

"Spells?" he frowns. "Are you epileptic or something?"

"More like psychometric."

He has to keep shifting his attention back and forth between Mozart, whom he's trying to feed, and me. "Sorry, what?"

I'm not even sure it's a real word. "Psychometry, have you ever heard of it?"

Once the kitten gets started, he sucks down the formula quickly. Hopper draws a second portion and works at getting the little guy to open his mouth again. "I think so. Isn't that where…"

He cuts his eyes back to me and I see understanding dawning on him. "Holy moly, seriously? You mean you get psychic hits from touching things?"

There. It's out. I sip more, and drop my gaze to the table. "The necklace you brought… when I touched it I saw… something. Felt what the last owner did when she wore it."

He sits back in mild shock, forgetting for a moment he's feeding Mozart, and drops his hand to his lap. Formula leaks out onto his jeans and the kitten mews. "No way."

The words are said with a type of soft reverence, as if this is the coolest thing he's ever heard. It gives me a small measure of hope.

I've heard the same said before in a sarcastic, flippant manner, but there's not a trace of any of that in his tone or his face when I look up.

"The woman who owned the necklace was really sick, I think. Some of her spirit is connected to those garnets."

He's still staring at me rather than Mozart. "You mean her ghost is attached to the necklace?"

Spirit communication isn't my strong suit, that'd be Winter's ability. "Seems to be. There's something unresolved about her death. She's anchored herself to that piece of jewelry. Or at least has some strong memories associated with it."

Hopper resumes feeding, then switches to Vivaldi. He tucks the tiny female against his chest, and she stops crying. He reloads the dropper and she eagerly begins to suck when he brings it to her mouth. "That's a good girl," he murmurs to her.

He needs time to process what I've just laid on him. At least he hasn't jumped up and run screaming from the shop.

I pick up a second dropper and start feeding St. Hildegard. We sit in silence, the sun warming us and the kittens
as we feed them.

Out of the blue, Hopper says, "I'm sorry."

Here it comes, I think. He's about to tell me he can't
handle the fact I have the Touch, I'm really a witch, or some
combination of *I don't believe in magick* and *you need to see a
psychiatrist*. I've heard all that and worse from those who
consider themselves normal.

That's why I don't talk about my gifts anymore. Sure,
some folks like to visit the shop and dabble in love potions,
tarot cards, astrology, and crystals, but when confronted
with someone who has real magick powers, psychic abilities, or practices hands-on healing, they chalk it off as
psychosis or the devil's work.

My heart breaks a little, and all I can do is nod. "It's
okay."

"I had no idea you're sensitive like that," he says. I feel
his weighty stare on me. "I would never have brought it if I'd
known Mrs. Fontaine's spirit was still connected and it'd
hurt you."

Wait. *What?* I meet his gaze and see that he actually does
understand. He's sorry for being the cause of what
happened, not sorry as in, *hey, you're crazy and I'll see later.*

"I should have told you," I confess. "I wasn't sure how
you'd take it."

He finishes with Vivaldi, and she slides off to sleep in his
big hand. He sets down the dropper and strokes her a
couple times before setting her in the box next to the
lavender scented teddy bear. He picks up Beethoven, whose
cry is the loudest of them all.

Settling the kitten against his belly, he begins feeding
him. "Like I said, we all have our secrets, Summer.

Granted, yours is a big one, but I'm glad you shared it with me."

Could he be any more perfect? I find myself smiling. "Me, too," I admit.

"So, you think there's something hinky about the woman's death?"

In my gut, I know there is. Just thinking about it makes my stomach revolt again. "I'm not sure what, but yes. I've never experienced something quite like that before."

"Does it happen a lot? You touch them and you get some kind of psychic info?"

"Not everything, nor all the time. It's kind of random. That's why I wear fingerless gloves a lot, even in the summer."

He grins. "I just thought that was part of your Stevie Nicks cool style."

I think I'm falling in love with this man. It feels good. "Thank you for not treating me like I'm some kind of freak."

"You *are* a freak." Still grinning, there's a teasing note in his voice. "But so am I. We can be freaks together, if you want."

Yes, I'm definitely falling in love with him.

This is bad, so, so bad. The vision from Beltane swims in front of my eyes...Hopper pushing a young boy on a swing. Smiling at someone I can't see, but who must be his wife.

I ignore the voice in my head telling me not to lead him on. He's not staying with me—the vision has shown me that. He's going to fall in love and marry another. Have kids with her.

Defiantly, I lift my chin and spurn fate. "I'd like that."

My stomach settles, and my heart fills with happiness. We finish feeding the kittens and then stare at them as they sleep, cuddled together.

"When you touch them," Hopper says quietly, "do you get a hit? Do you know what happened to their mother? Who brought them to the shop this morning?"

"No, but it doesn't matter. They're here. We have to take care of them."

He nods. "And Mrs. Fontaine's death? Is that something we have to look into?"

I like how he says *we*. It's my turn to nod. "In my vision, she wasn't much older than twenty-seven. Maybe thirty? Too young to die, that's for sure. Did she have cancer or something?"

He frowns. "Nah, she was older than that. I don't remember exactly, but I'm pretty sure she was at least in her sixties."

This doesn't jive with what I saw and felt, but perhaps the necklace was showing me something in the distant past, rather than recent. All I know is it had a taint of magick, and a whole lot of fear wrapped up in it.

"I need to find out for sure if it's her, and if there's any way I can help her."

He rises from the chair, takes a sip of the tea, and makes a face. "What is that?"

"Ginger." I laugh at his expression. "It settles the stomach."

He's still making a face as he asks, "What about your client this afternoon? Are we still taking water to her?"

Right now, I just want to be with him. But if there's a way to help Mrs. Sorensen relieve her arthritis pain, I'll do it.

Healing may not be my strongest gift, but I do what I can. "You bet we are."

*W*hen we arrive with multiple five-gallon buckets from the hot spring, we're met at the door by her live-in caretaker, Linda.

Hopper insisted on driving his truck, and I know this is partially because he wants to take care of me and he's a control freak when it comes to driving. He's asked three times on the way to Mrs. Sorensen's if I'm sure I'm okay and don't need to go to the ER.

Thanks to Spring's magick, I feel fine. I brought a travel mug of her ginger iced tea and my stomach is completely normal, even hungry.

A part of me wants to ask Hopper out to eat after we're done here, but there's also a part of me that's scared to. I'm torn between wanting to pursue this relationship, and knowing no good can come of it.

The house is in a ritzy upscale neighborhood. Our little town consists of eleven thousand people, and there are more in the poverty range than Mrs. Sorensen's upper-class division.

The entryway is two stories tall with a large chandelier

hanging from the high ceiling. Various antiques line the walls. There's a room to the left and one to the right—the door to the former is closed and I can see a sitting room in the latter. A grand staircase leads upstairs, and I figure her bedroom is there, but she told me she had a temporary bedroom on the first floor, since her hips don't like the climb.

Linda is not surprised at our arrival—I called ahead to let them know we were coming. She does seem slightly annoyed, as if this is foolish. I suppose to her, it is.

The hot spring on our land has healing water, and anyone who has experienced it knows it works. We don't open it to the public, but we allow certain people who need healing assistance to make use of it. I wish I could share it with the whole world and heal everyone.

The house is well air conditioned, but Linda appears to be sweating. "I'll tell Mrs. Sorensen you're here," she tells us. She points to the sitting room. "Have a seat."

She goes to a door on the left, disappearing inside and closing it behind her.

Hopper says in a low voice, "Fancy digs. You know, the Fontaine's is just down the block."

"Really?" We walk toward the sitting room and I admire the expensive furniture, beautiful rugs and drapes, and the large fireplace with a marble mantle. "Do you think you could take me there after we're done?"

Hopper eyes an antique rocking chair and table near the window which looks over the drive. I see how he examines the delicate scroll work on it and checks out how it is put together. "Sure. The house is going up for sale, I heard. Guess her husband's leaving town."

Linda returns to escort us to see Mrs. Sorensen. I'm shocked to see her in bed looking pale.

She reaches out a hand to me and smiles. "I'm so glad you came, Summer. I'm sorry I'm not up and about."

She's in her late sixties, but I swear she's aged ten years overnight. Of course, I haven't seen her in a couple weeks. "Is there something besides your arthritis keeping you in bed?"

"The doctors don't know what's wrong with me." She waves a thin, boney hand in the air, as if it's nothing to worry about. "Who is this handsome young man with you?"

I make introductions, and she flatters Hopper, making him smile. I swear I can see the lightest blush on his cheeks.

"Where would you like me to haul the water?" he asks her.

"There's a bathroom with a tub just down the hall. Have Linda show you."

He takes off to get the buckets out of his truck. I hold Mrs. Sorensen's hand. "I'll heat it for you so it won't be cold when you get in."

The older woman knows about my spellwork, and the fact my hands can be useful tools on occasion. Often times I warm them to place on her sore joints. She gives me another weak smile "You truly are full service, and I appreciate it."

Not long after, Linda has her soaking. Hopper and I wait again in the sitting room. His eye for antiques has him inventorying some of the more special pieces, telling me all about them.

I'm examining a family picture on the mantle when the front door flies open and a well-dressed woman storms in. "Mother?" She heads to the left and the empty bedroom, returning when she realizes no one is in there. "Mother! Where are you?"

She spots us and marches in. "Who are you?"

I introduce myself and Hopper and explain about the water.

She stares at me with a blank look on her face. "Spring water?"

"It helps your mother's arthritis. She regularly comes to our shop, Conjure, and takes a bath in the hot spring there." The woman's hair is pulled up in a severe bun. Her makeup is heavy, and she's wearing expensive jewelry along with designer clothes.

She shrugs off the couture handbag from her shoulder and laughs. "And just how much are you charging for this healing water?" The way she says it lets me know she thinks this is a joke. That I'm taking her mother for a ride, making her believe it can help her aching joints.

"I'm not. She's my friend, not just a client, and the minerals are well documented to reduce inflammation and increase blood flow. I know she's having health issues, and I thought this might make her feel better."

Mrs. Sorensen is a generous client. I never charge her for dips and yet I always end up finding an extra hundred tucked somewhere in my treatment room after she's been there. I know they come from her, even though I've never caught her slipping it there. She's a strong believer in energy healing. Her crystal collection rivals mine, and that's saying something.

But obviously, her daughter does not share her belief in alternative medicine.

Mrs. Sorensen has told me about both of her daughters, Roberta and Maxine. I'm guessing this is Roberta. She's a lawyer in Eugene. "What my mother needs to feel better is none of your concern. She's seen several qualified experts and has medication."

Linda appears in the doorway. "Oh, Mrs. Powell. We weren't expecting you."

"This is my home. I don't need to make an appointment, do I?"

Linda pales slightly, taking a step back and wiping sweat from her brow. "Your mother is bathing. She'll be out in a little bit."

"I need to speak to her now. I have to get back to the office."

I step forward, knowing better than to argue or intervene, but unable to stop myself. "It would be best if she soaks for another fifteen to twenty minutes."

Roberta whirls on me. "Linda, see these people to the door."

I can see Linda's annoyance at being seen as nothing more than hired help. I assume she has some kind of nursing background, and bottom line, she's a healer, too. But like Roberta, she believes traditional medicine is best.

"Come on, Hopper," I say. "Linda, please tell Mrs. Sorensen we said goodbye, and she's to call me if she needs anything."

Hopper and I pass Roberta and Linda moves as we exit the sitting room. From behind us, Roberta calls, "My mother won't be contacting you. If she needs anything, I'll help her."

I grit my teeth. Hopper and I don't say anything to each other until we're in his truck.

"You did a good thing, Summer." He pats my arm. "Don't let that woman get to you."

Inside, I'm furious, my inner fire blazing. Obviously traditional medicine is not helping Mrs. Sorensen. What can soaking in some spring water hurt?

"I was hoping to do energy work on her before we left. I hate that she's in such bad shape. She was doing fairly well a couple weeks ago. Today, she looks like death warmed over. If I could've checked her chakras, I might've figured out what's going on."

He squeezes my arm. "You did what you could."

Did I? Maybe I should have insisted on sticking around until Mrs. Sorensen was out of the bath. That might have ended up in a fight with Roberta, maybe even Linda, but right now I'm kind of itching for one. "I'll phone her later and see if there's anything else I can do."

"Still wanna drive by the Fontaine's?"

Since I can't help Mrs. Sorensen any further at the moment, I might as well look into Mariel Fontaine and see if I can get more information about her. I probably should let it go, but I can't. "Yes, let's do it."

Hopper puts the truck into gear. "After that, do you want to get an early dinner?"

Shyness swamps me again. I shoot him a glance. "I would love to."

5

_T_he Fontaine house is a mansion.

It even has a wrought iron fence around the outside of the property, and as Hopper drives onto the grounds, a prickling sensation covers my skin. It feels like a thousand cold needles poking me.

A magickal ward. Immediately, I wonder who put it up and what they're trying to keep out.

On the way over, I looked up Mariel's obituary on my phone. Hopper is correct—she was sixty-three when she passed. In the picture with the obit, she looks to be in her thirties.

I'm the first to use rose water, rose quartz, and mookaite jasper to keep my looks as wrinkle-free as possible, but Mariel must've tapped into the fountain of youth.

As we cruise down the long drive, I'm slightly surprised to see the gate open. I admire the beautiful plantings on both sides of the lane and think how much Spring would love this. The roses are in full bloom, and there are lush, green plants interspersed between the bushes.

The drive curves in an arch in front of the grand two-story brick home, complete with four large white pillars. The porch is several feet off the ground with a wide sweeping staircase. There are more flowers and plants around the foundation, and concrete planters filled with overflowing ferns and white geraniums lining the steps.

I recognize a few of the plants along the foundation—foxglove, wolfsbane, belladonna, and some nightshade. Those are strong magick in and of themselves.

Maybe that's what I was picking up on in the vision—Mariel was a witch.

Two cars are parked at the foot of the grand staircase, one with a magnetic sign on the side stating it belongs to Holly Dunn, real estate agent. The second, a gold colored Mercedes Benz, is parked several feet behind it.

In the middle of the big oval drive is a water fountain with a naked cherub in the center, pouring water from an urn over his shoulder.

The landscaping alone probably costs more than our entire shop. Hopper pulls behind the Mercedes and parks. "Looks like the house is open for a tour. Wanna have a look?"

"The potential buyers might not like us crashing their party," I say, then grin. "Let's do it."

This could be my one chance to figure out if something doesn't add up in Mariel's death. Hopefully, I can sense whatever I felt when I held the necklace. There is still the hint of something from it telling me there's more to it than what people believe.

Between the wards and the assortment of magickal herbs and flowers, I'm guessing she was definitely into magick.

If I can get inside and touch something that belonged to her, I might get another hit. The problem is, it could also knock me out like her necklace did. I'll have to be extra careful.

"We need a cover," Hopper says, "and we better hope the realtor doesn't recognize us."

"I've never heard of her, so I doubt she's one of our clients."

"I don't know her either," he says. "We'll pretend we're from out of town, just a couple interested in the house."

A couple? "Works for me."

We exchange a conspiratorial smile and bail from the truck. As we climb the steps the prickling sensation grows, and I lower my voice. "All I really need is to pick up the energy in the house, maybe get close to her bedroom. I may not even need to touch anything, and I don't want to pass out on you like I did earlier."

"How about you don't touch anything at all? This is simply a scouting expedition to see what we can find out, okay?"

He's right to be conservative. "Good call. I'll keep my hands in my pockets."

"I'd appreciate that. You scared the devil out of me earlier. I don't need a repeat."

I don't either. But I can feel a tug at my own magick, like Mariel urging me on.

We stop at the door and look at each other. "Should we ring the doorbell or just walk in?" Hopper asks.

"Beats me. If we're crashing, we might as well do it up right. Let's walk in and see what happens. As big as this place is, we may get in and out before anyone even notices."

He grins. "I like the way you operate."

The house is quiet, cavernous. Every light is on. The air is cooler than outside, but still oppressively humid.

The entry itself seems to go on for a mile, two large

winding staircases that meet overhead, multiple chandeliers and two large rooms are on each side. Most of the furniture is gone and the walls look bare without any photos or paintings. I hear muffled voices in a distant wing, but they're too far away to understand.

The warding is stronger, but I see very few items suggesting a witch lived here. There are no obviously magickal items on display. Perhaps they were sold.

We glance in the various rooms—formal living room, dining room, guest bathroom—then Hopper points a finger at the stairs. Understanding his nonverbal cue, I follow him. Mariel's bedroom is probably on the second floor.

The stairs are thickly carpeted, the wood handrailing stained a rich walnut. Hopper takes the lead, climbing carefully, as though expecting them to creak and give us away.

I sort of feel like a kid sneaking around as we come to the top of the stairs and the second-floor landing. There are multiple bedrooms, a study, and a huge library. I could spend hours in the last, even though it looks like someone has helped themselves to certain sections and removed several collections. Maybe some were sold like the titles Hopper bought.

I'm eyeing a beautiful globe by the desk and a telescope by the window when he makes a *psst* noise.

At the end of the hall, he leads me into a large bedroom suite. There's still plenty of furniture here, including a four-poster bed, dressing table, and two Queen Anne chairs in front of a fireplace.

There's an elegant standing mirror in one corner, a reading nook in the other. A comfortable chair in the reading area has an ornate side table with three books on it, the top edition open with a bookmark lying inside. A blanket is draped over the arm of the chair, as if the owner is about to return any moment, kick her feet up onto the stool and resume her place.

I peruse it and note the subject is the Salem witch trials. Interesting. I drop to my knees and check under the bed and am rewarded for my efforts. A large circle with various protection sigils is drawn on the floorboards.

Mariel knew she was in danger. She was trying to protect herself, but from whom or what?

Hopper watches me carefully. I rise and he gives me a questioning look. "Are you getting anything?" he whispers.

I want to touch that circle, but it's infused with very strong magick, and I'd probably pass out. I survey the room for something less strong. "A little," I tell him.

I step closer to the dressing table and admire a silver brush and a hand mirror. There's a collection of perfume bottles and a framed photograph of a young Mariel in sepia tones. Funny, because the format suggests it was taken in the nineteen twenties or thirties. Maybe its her grand-mother. If so, she's nearly her clone.

The only other explanation is Mariel's protection spells were keeping old age away as well.

A writing desk near the window has more photos. Babies, none over the age of a year. Her obituary mentioned she and her husband, Kaan, lost three infant children.

I feel a sharp pain in my chest, seeing their faces, and tears well in my eyes and my hand goes to my heart. I want a child so badly, it's as if I can feel her pain echoing within these walls. Grief for her, as well as the babies who didn't get to grow up, drills its way into my soul.

A warm hand on my shoulder brings me out of my emotional hole. I find Hopper standing next to me, concern edging his features. "Are you okay?"

Swallowing down the sorrow and blinking the tears

from my eyes, I give him a curt nod. I turn from the desk and the sad pictures and draw a ragged breath.

As promised, I keep my hands in my pockets and simply try to pick up the energy in the room. Several of the walls are covered with beautiful floral wallpaper, and the bedspread and curtains are of the highest quality. Mariel liked beauty and comfort, and the room is definitely feminine, even though her obituary said her husband was still alive. Did he sleep here or in a separate bedroom?

My attention is drawn to the garden outside the window as a bird flies by. I see Greek statues, hedgerows, and more plants and herbs.

Everything radiates out from a center section that contains a wide stone table. Someone has placed planters with ferns and trailing vines on each end. As I study the layout, it's obvious there are five apple trees planted at hexagonal angles surrounding the table. An altar?

I close my eyes and ask her spirit to direct me to anything I need to know or investigate. When I open them, I look to the left and feel my feet propelled toward the double closet doors.

Opening them, I have to flip on the light to see inside the room that's nearly as big as my entire cabin. There are two overhead chandeliers, beautiful shelves filled with designer shoes and handbags everywhere. Racks of expensive clothes. Another full-length mirror, and several upholstered stools. Again, extremely feminine, not a hint of a male presence.

Everything appears to be in its place, nothing moved or missing, and once again I wonder why this stuff wasn't included in the estate sale. She has no children to benefit from the items and there was no mention of extended family, such as a sister who might make use of it. Perhaps her husband simply can't part with the items yet. Her passing was only a week ago.

Across from the mirror, I notice a large picture draped with a silk cloth covering whatever's underneath. Lifting one corner, I see an oil painting, but it's difficult to see the details. As if he can read my mind, Hopper joins me and reaches to the top to draw the silk aside.

For a moment, we're both speechless, then he says, "Yikes. That's not too creepy."

Wow is right. The oil painting is of a naked woman lying on a raised altar, a man in a robe standing over her. A shudder of knowing goes over me.

"Is that...?" Hopper tilts his head to look closer at the woman's face.

"Yes," I say, "and that altar is in the garden."

"Altar?" He clears his throat. "The guy is holding a knife."

It's a ceremonial athame and a shiver runs over my skin. I have a feeling the man in the picture is Kaan Fontaine, and even with the hood, I'm sure he's the man in my vision.

"Let's get out of here."

Before Hopper can replace the cloth, a deep and sinister voice asks, "What are you doing in here?"

6

*T*he voice belongs to a man blocking our escape. He's a distinguished looking older gentleman with silver streaks in his dark hair and goatee. His eyes are obsidian flakes, hard and glinting. Although he's just under six foot, he carries the confident stature of someone bigger.

Kaan Fontaine.

Startled, Hopper, who froze in the act of fixing the silk cloth, jerks back. This causes the entire cover to fall to the floor at our feet. "Oopsy," he says softly.

A woman appears behind Mr. Fontaine and gives a disconcerted gasp when she sees the portrait.

"I'm so sorry." I step forward to shield Hopper as best as I can. Fontaine is definitely a man of magick—black magick. It oozes off him and creeps its way toward me.

He's not even trying to hide it, quite honestly. He reminds me of a stereotypical magician—the kind that performs stage tricks with that goatee and haughty look.

"My husband and I came from Eugene to visit friends," I tell them. "They said this place was for sale, and since we have a love for old Victorian mansions, I begged Big Daddy here to bring me by so I could see it. Someone mentioned there was going to be an open house later today, but when we saw the gates open and your cars parked outside, we thought we'd just stop in. Unfortunately, we have to leave town today, and can't make the open house. I hope you understand."

I'm babbling, but I suck at lying and this is what happens. Seeing the expressions on both of their faces, I press my lips together and send a protective bubble over both me and Hopper.

"Are you interested in buying?" The realtor, Holly, glances back and forth between us.

Fontaine studies us, too, but I can see he doesn't believe my little story.

Before I can answer, Hopper grabs my hand—not by the palm, but the fingers—and brings my knuckles to his lips, giving them a little kiss. "We're always in the market for these old places. They have such character." He lies easily, drawing me beside him toward the door. "Not sure I want to live in such a small town. But the little lady likes the quaint atmosphere."

I almost want to laugh because this *little lady* is about to get Hopper in a lot of trouble.

Electricity pops and sizzles in the air. I wonder if I'm the only one who feels it. When I glance at Hopper, I realize he and Fontaine are locked in some kind of male domination thing, staring each other down.

I fake a smile. "It really is a stunning house," I say, "but I think it's a little big for us."

I push Hopper toward the exit, hoping our intruders let us pass. "We best be going, Big Daddy."

Holly graciously steps out of the way, but Fontaine

doesn't. Before I can skirt him, he holds out a hand. "I'm the owner, Kaan Fontaine. I didn't catch your name."

Not only do I intend to never give it to him, I also won't shake hands with him.

I put my hand over my mouth and cough. "Sorry, I have a cold. Very contagious."

Once more, I try to edge around him but he's not having it. "If you'd like a tour, I'd be happy to show you the rest of the house myself."

Hopper reaches out and pats him on the shoulder. "Not necessary. We have to get going."

I could be mistaken, but I swear Hopper gives Kaan a little physical encouragement. At the same time, he guides me out of the closet. We make haste to the bedroom door, but before we get more than a few feet, Holly holds out a card, following on our heels. "Please reach out if you decide you'd like to make an offer."

Hopper takes it, so I don't have to—*good man*—and we take the hallway toward the stairs. I feel those obsidian eyes on my back, and I give a little push with my magick to let Mr. Fontaine know I have no interest in playing games with him.

As we hustle down the stairs, however, I feel like I have a target on me.

I hear his thoughts in the back of my mind. *I know who you are, little witch.*

Hopper and I can't get outside fast enough, and I'm sweating by the time we jump in his truck. The heat inside is even worse, suffocating, and as soon as he turns the key, the air conditioning kicks in, sending a wave of more hot air over my skin.

I feel slightly dizzy until I reinforce my bubble. The sensation of Kaan's black magick slides off me. It's unnervingly akin to what I feel when I pick up my mother's vintage hand mirror.

"Well, that was interesting," Hopper says as we barrel down the drive.

The prickly sensation of the ward is icy hot on my skin, but it falls away the moment we cross the property line onto the street. It's only then that I breathe a sigh of relief.

The now cooler air caresses me. In my mind's eye, I imagine flooding the truck with white light, extending my bubble of protection as far as I can. I can't wait to get to the shop and run selenite through my aura.

"How are you doing, Little Lady?"

I look over to see Hopper grinning. I feel nearly normal, simply from his smile. "Just fine, Big Daddy."

We both break out laughing, releasing pent up energy.

"You're good," he says. "Quick on your feet. Now I know who to call next time I need a partner in crime."

"Mr. Fontaine didn't believe a word I said. You may want to rethink that."

Hopper shrugs and gives another laugh. "So, what do you think happened to Mariel? Any clue?"

Remembering the feel of Kaan's eyes, I shudder. "Black magick."

"Seriously? Is that what killed her?"

"I can't say for sure, but it's possible. I have an idea— maybe we can discuss it over dinner?"

He heads downtown. "I'm at your service. What's your favorite place?"

We end up at the best joint in town. Over gigantic slices of cheese pizza and bucket sodas, I ask him about the estate sale and what else he bought.

"A mid-century telephone table, a couple chairs, and the two boxes of jewelry. Those books for Spring, and some for me. I like to read weird things, like myths and legends."

"Do you still have all the jewelry?"

He nods and swallows a mouthful of pizza. "I have to inventory it before I can put it in the store."

Perfect. It's risky, but I might be able to get some answers to my questions. "Mind if I take a look at it after we're done here?"

"Not at all." He eyes me speculatively. "You're not scared about...you know...the black magick? Curses or hexes or whatever that dude is into?"

"I'd be an idiot not to be, but if he caused Mariel's death, I need to prove it."

"What can you do about it? It's not like you can report him to Chief MacGregor, right?"

Tristan knows there have been other deaths in Raven Falls that are the result of magick. Explaining that to Hopper is for another day. "One step at a time, Big Daddy," I tease. "One step at a time."

We eat in companionable silence for the next several minutes. "I'm sorry you had to be away from your shop all day," I tell him.

"No worries. I was supposed to film a segment for my Hopping Antiques channel, but I can do it later."

Hopper's found a niche with people online who enjoy antiquing and finding rare pieces. He's quite knowledge-able about mid-century items, and he tells me it's a hot market right now for them. "What's the segment on?" I ask.

"Toasters," he says, totally serious.

I make a face. "Riveting, I'm sure."

"For some, it is. I recently came across a guy in California with quite a collection. There's one 1960s vintage

Smeg he's missing and guess what I found on my last expedition north?"

He often heads into Canada to look for unique items. Other times he heads east to Wyoming, or Idaho, and occasionally as far as the Badlands. He's always on the hunt, and I think that's what keeps his life interesting. I envy all the traveling he does.

"Never heard of such a thing, but I hope the guy is willing to pay a pretty penny for it," I say with a grin.

"He is, but I want to do a segment on it for my fans before I sell it to him."

It's hard for me to wrap my mind around the fact Hopper may be a millionaire because of his antiques obsession. He doesn't talk about his family or past, and although he was in the military for a while, he doesn't strike me as the type to go to war.

I don't really care where his money came from, or what he does with it, but I do love seeing the modern metal sculptures he makes in his workshop in the barn behind his store. They're raw and beautiful, and they litter his property. He doesn't sell them, claiming they're for his enjoyment only.

When we finally get back, it's late. We sit in his truck a moment, and he takes a phone call. A customer is at his place, wanting to buy something. As he talks to the guy, and assures him he'll be there in a few minutes, I see a vision.

Hopper leaning across to kiss me.

Okay, maybe it's just my active imagination, but I like believing it's the future.

I let it play out, not surprised when I see myself return the kiss, then crawl into his lap to do more.

"I can walk you in." He snaps me out of my day dreaming. Apparently, his call is over. "We may have to do the jewelry thing tomorrow, though. I forgot I promised this guy

47

I'd stay open late so he could buy an antique dresser for his wife's birthday tomorrow."

I feel like a teenager on her first date. Heat rises into my cheeks at the fact I want to ravish him in his truck. "Oh, that's okay. I'll see you tomorrow."

He jumps out and rushes over to open my door. I climb out, feeling that awkward embarrassment again. "Thank you. I...you know, for everything. It was awesome. Amazing."

I press my lips together, so I quit talking. Why can't I be cool and casual like Autumn is? She seems to always find the right words to say.

He grins and puts his hands in his pockets. "Are you sure you don't need help with the kittens tonight? I can come back later."

We're putting off saying goodbye, and again I'm reminded of teenagers. I want to reach out and touch his arm so badly, I nearly do it. Godfrey appears and lets out a loud meow that sounds like, *gross humans.*

It's all the distraction I need. I keep my hands to myself. "I'll call if I need help, I promise."

This seems to appease him, and he nods.

"Goodnight," I say and start to walk away.

Hopper grabs hold of my elbow and pulls me back to him. He stares into my eyes for a long moment and I know what's about to happen.

Score one for this vision.

But I sense his hesitation, his worry I might freak out if he does it.

Shyness gone, I reach up and slide one of my gloved hands behind his neck, bringing his lips to mine.

I make it a point to leave no doubt in his mind that I do very much want to be kissed.

—————

7

*L*ips still buzzing, I ditch my stuff and take over for Autumn.

Hopper and I made plans to meet tomorrow after my last appointment. That way he'll be able to keep his store open for customers and get his video done.

I bring back the leftover pizza to share with my sisters and thank them for filling in for me.

Spring is holding a class, but other than that, there are few customers. Godfrey makes himself at home in the center of the crafting table to the women's delight. The kittens are sleeping in the office where Winter is working on the books.

"Thank the goddess you're here," she says when I enter, then she points at the kittens. "I'm not cut out for this mothering thing. I had to change the blanket three times. They're peeing and pooping machines." She gives an exaggerated shudder.

"Did you know there's a black magick sorcerer in Raven Falls? A dark wizard?"

She eases back in the padded office chair. "I've heard

rumors, but never confirmed it. From the sounds of it, he must keep a low profile."

"His name is Kaan Fontaine. His wife died a week or so ago, but there are things about her death that don't add up."

She swings a leg over the other. "Did you see him during your episode this morning? Is that how you figured it out?"

"Sort of. The necklace belongs to his wife, and I saw him when I touched it. At least I think it was him. He was quite a bit younger than the man I met today. I think he and Mariel have been around a lot longer than they appear."

I tell her about the ward and the painting, as well as the protection ward she had under her bed. "Do you think you can help me find out if magick killed her?"

"Dangerous stuff, Summer. Are you sure you want to go there?"

"Hopper's bringing two boxes of Mariel's jewelry over tomorrow. I'm going to see what kind of hits I get off them. That'll determine if I take it further."

"Well then, I best throw up some extra protection," she says. "I don't want this Mr. Fontaine paying us a visit."

"Thank you. I was also wondering if you could reach out and contact Mariel's ghost. Maybe she can tell us what's going on."

My sister doesn't look all that excited about contacting the woman's spirit, but then again, Winter doesn't look excited about anything. "Do you still have the necklace?"

"Yes, do you want me to get it?"

"I need to finish the books right now. Let's meet after closing in the kitchen."

The crafting class runs over by ten minutes, and I help Spring clean up as we see everyone out. We retreat to the kitchen where Winter is waiting. She has the kettle heating on the stove, knowing Spring will want a cup. Honestly, after the day I've had, I could use a gallon of coffee, but some of Spring's organic peppermint tea will have to do.

Autumn is watching the kittens in her client room, and Spring retrieves a few of the leftover bakery items from the front case for us to munch on.

I carry the bowl with the necklace to the table and put it in front of Winter. She's reading a book Hopper brought.

"Did you know one of the lost native tribes actually had a book made from animal skins with stories written in it?" We both shake our heads and she goes on. "This journal references it, but claims no one could read the thing because the language was lost with that tribe. There was a woman in the colony who seemed to have the ability to translate, but the man who wrote this journal didn't believe she knew what she was doing. At the time this was written, the general consensus was that it was some type of instruction manual on how to deal with an angry spirit."

She smiles, that subject close to her heart.

After everything that's happened today, I have trouble shifting my mind to the underlying subject matter she's referring to. The monster imprisoned on the land deep inside the earth is always a topic of conversation between us these days. We believe our mother is somehow bound to it. Spring has been on a quest to break that binding and destroy the thing.

I don't understand how this piece of trivia could help, but since we have no solid leads as to what to do about "the master," I guess everything feels like a piece of hope. "What happened to this manual?"

She flips to a particular entry and taps the page with her finger. "He referenced it as the lost tribe's Book of the Dead. I looked it up on the internet, but the only mention I could find was to something in one of the natural history museums in Eugene. They don't call it that, but they reference it by number, and it might be the same thing."

I eat one of the oatmeal raisin cookies Spring placed on the table. She brings over a teapot and pours each of us a cup. Winter ignores hers—she prefers coffee—but I blow on the hot tea and enjoy the uplifting smell. Spring always tells us peppermint tea can solve any problem, but so far, it hasn't solved the one with our mother's soul.

And I'm worried there is no solving that problem if she was dabbling in black magick.

"Too bad it can't help us with Mom," Spring says, as if she's reading my mind.

Winter ignores her but snatches up a cookie. "If only someone could read it. It may reference our demon and give us a clue on how to get rid of the thing."

"Wait," I say, "What your reading is a diary?"

Winter shows me the inside page. "It belonged to a naturalist named A. Henson. He explored the coastline in the 1600s. It's full of notes and drawings. Looks to me like this should be in the museum, too, since it contains so much information about this area at that time."

I gingerly touch the edges and don't get any weird hits, so I flip through it, seeing what Winter is talking about. The man's beautiful script, along with various sketches of fauna, insects, and animals, looks like a natural history book in and of itself.

Winter takes a hairband off her wrist and rakes her crazy curls into a sloppy ponytail. "Okay, let's get started."

Spring and I watch as she pulls the bowl toward her. She takes off the protection bracelets of hematite and onyx I made for her, and sets them on the table. Closing her eyes, she breathes deeply. I know she's working on retracting her wards that keep the spirits at bay. If she didn't protect herself, she'd see them everywhere, and have them constantly chattering at her and demanding her help.

After she's opened the channel to the other side, she reaches for the necklace, hesitantly touching the garnet and metal. I stare, willing it to be the conduit between Winter and Mariel.

As my eyes focus on the gemstones. I feel that tugging in my breastbone. I'm not even touching it, but I can feel the magick beginning to roll off the snake.

It seems to shimmer and for a brief second, I swear the garnet eyes come alive. The head tilts slightly and zeros in on Winter's hand. I jump up, knocking it to the table. "No!"

Tea splashes over the edges of our cups, and I knock my cookie to the floor, the pieces going in all directions. Winter looks up startled. Spring grips the table that's still shaking.

"What is it?" Winter huffs.

"Didn't you see it?" I say. "It... it turned into a snake."

My sisters look at me as if I'm the one who's grown a snake's head. "It is a snake," Spring reminds me, gripping my hand and giving it a squeeze. "But it's not real. Do you think your nerves are getting to you?"

"I...I saw it come to life."

Winter glances at the necklace and back to me. "I didn't see it change."

I rub my eyes and slowly resume my seat, as Spring grabs a dishtowel to mop up the tea.

Once she's done, I ask Winter, "Did you have a connection to Mariel?"

She shakes her head. "I'll try again, okay?"

"What if it's cursed? Will it hurt you?"

She gives me a lopsided grin. "You're the expert on those, sister. What do you think?"

I think my oldest sibling is one tough cookie, but black

magick is nothing to fool with. "We need to be extra cautious."

"I agree," Winter says. "What do you suggest? I don't have to touch it, but it would help."

I've already held that thing, maybe that's why I can see the magick suspended in it now. But Winter touched it too, and she didn't see anything other than a piece of costume jewelry with a couple gemstones in it.

I'm tired, and it's been a long day. Maybe Spring is right about my nerves. "Try it without touching the necklace. I just don't trust it."

Winter and Spring exchange a look I ignore. Spring holds my hand as Winter once more does her thing and reaches out to the spirit world.

Silence falls over us and Winter seems completely at ease, but I feel like grinding my teeth. I want to know what happened to Mariel, and if there's something I need to do to help her. On the other hand, black magick scares me and I want nothing to do with it. I certainly don't want to put my sisters in danger, and I'm already worried I've done that.

That *Mom* has done that.

Minutes pass, and Winter closes her eyes. That quiet calm she always gets when interacting with the spirit world comes over her and I can't help but relax somewhat myself. I try not to stare at the necklace, and trust that Winter won't do anything that'd put herself in danger.

Usually crossing the veil and connecting with a certain spirit comes easy to her, and I wonder why it's taking so long tonight.

Worry and doubt continue to creep in, a layer of fear riding my skin. I'm about to tell her to quit, to return to our side where I can protect her, when she opens her eyes.

She's staring across the room, but I can tell she's not

seeing Spring's collection of pie birds on the shelf. "Is she here?" I whisper.

Winter doesn't answer, doesn't even blink. "Not exactly."

Even though neither Spring nor I can see or hear spirits for the most part, we look behind us.

"What do you mean?" I ask Winter.

"I can see her, but she seems to be behind a wall. She's talking and trying to get through it, I just can't understand what she's saying."

"What kind?" Spring wants to know.

Winter heaves a sigh. "A wall of magick."

Winter finally releases Mariel's spirit, and the three of us spend the next twenty minutes discussing what the wall might mean and how to deal with the necklace. We decide to bury it in one of Spring's gardens to see if we can release the negative energy.

I bring the kittens home with me, Cinders flying overhead as I walk the path in the growing darkness. At my cabin, I give him his evening meal and take the kittens inside to feed them.

The runt, Mozart, seems less vocal than the others tonight. I fall asleep in my rocking chair holding him, and dream of fighting a man in a hooded cape surrounded by snakes.

I get up at one point and go to my private collection of crystals, pulling out all the black tourmaline, placing it around the doors and windows. I take my selenite wand and run it over myself and the kittens. I hear Godfrey prowling outside, and make him come in. I run the wand over his aura as well and endure his criticism about how unscientific crystal healing is.

Around two a.m., I can't get Mozart to eat, and fear grips

me. I try everything—including a few spells—pacing the floor as I cuddle and talk to him.

As if Autumn senses my mental anguish, she shows up at my doorstep. We take turns rubbing the little guy's belly and back, chant charms over him, and Autumn even sings as she carries him around my house.

Her voice is so much like our mother's, I sit and listen, memories of my childhood putting me to sleep.

We take turns with the kittens, and by five, we're exhausted, but Mozart is eating again and we're relieved. My sister and I sleep for a few hours before we have to get up and start our day.

8

----

*T*he next evening, I move the kittens behind the counter and take Autumn's place. Hopper will be by in an hour.

I confirm my appointments for the next day, feed the kittens, check for comments on the blog and YouTube channel, and update the website with the new crystal necklaces that came in over the weekend.

At nine on the dot, closing time, Hopper appears with his boxes. I close up and we carry everything to my cabin. The evening air is thick with humidity, the sound of toads and crickets filling the air. Nothing is moving, and I sense a thunderstorm coming in from the Pacific soon.

Cinders sits on his perch, head tucked under one wing as we arrive, and I'm suddenly self-conscious about Hopper seeing my cabin. He's never been inside, and I can't remember its condition, quite honestly. When you live alone, you don't worry much about appearances, and even when my friends come over, they're lucky if I've run the dust cloth around.

"Nice place." Hopper says, and I see he means it, putting me at ease.

I don't have air conditioning, so it's quite warm, but I open several windows to the cooling evening air. Amazingly, no matter how humid it gets during the day, it drops considerably at night. I believe it has to do with the fact we're surrounded by pine trees. Between the forest and the hot springs, the temperature is usually fairly moderate from spring through fall.

"Would you like something to drink?"

He declines and I'm slightly glad, since the most I have is tap water and a couple tins of Spring's tea blends.

I have plenty of crystals, and odds and ends of furniture, but not a lot else. Out of us four, Spring is the homemaker, and we usually meet at her place or in the Conjure kitchen for family gatherings. I'm a little more bohemian, and not prepared for company.

I collect several scarves and a deck of my oracle cards off the sofa and offer Hopper a seat. He pulls the coffee table close and puts the box on it. I carry the two shoe box size containers of jewelry and set those next to it.

"Is it safe to do this here?" he asks. "Maybe you should lie down before you try to get one of those vision thingies."

It's a good idea. "I will. First, I want to look at what you brought and see if anything stands out. We appreciate the books, by the way. Winter was looking at one earlier—it's a journal—and there's some amazing natural history about this area in it."

He seems pleased. "I kind of wanted to save that for myself, but figured I could borrow it once you guys are done reading it."

Such a generous soul. I stare at him, lost in those gray eyes and handsome face. I suddenly want to be better in the homemaking department, like Spring. I want to share my cabin with someone, discuss what we're making for dinner, do things couples do.

I send a silent prayer to Hestia, asking for help. I'm still torn, knowing Hopper deserves someone who can give him a family, and that's the one thing I won't relent on. Besides, there's the vision of him with another woman and kids.

I sigh. "Did you grow up around here?"

"Northern California. You?"

"Born and raised in Raven Falls. We all lived in Winter's cabin. It was our parents and is the largest."

"Must be nice," he says. "We moved around a lot, never really put down roots. Then I left and joined the Marines. More years of wandering."

"Do you feel settled here?"

He looks at the kittens and gives a small smile. "More so every day."

"I envy you. I've always wanted to travel," I tell him. "Don't get me wrong, I love it here. Raven Falls isn't perfect, but there are worse places, I suppose. It's just... I've never lived anywhere else. Never even went away to college. There's so much of the world I want to see."

"Why don't we go see some of it, then?" He makes a gesture with his hands like it's no big deal. "Where do you want to go? Maybe I've been there. I can be your tour guide."

I laugh. "I know it's rather cliché, but have you been to Paris? I'd love to go there."

"*Mais oui, mademoiselle.*" His French accent is awful, making me laugh even more. "And there's Rome and Vienna. I've been there, too. You'll love Paris, but I suggest we skip Rome and hit Milan. A little more laid-back and the food is better."

Off in the distance, I hear the boom of thunder. A breeze

picks up, blowing my curtains from the open windows. "You've really been to those cities?"

"I have, and I'm happy to take you to see them anytime."

Oh Hestia, I need a lot of help. I'm dying to ask if he wants a family, because what if he doesn't? What if he really *is* the perfect man for me?

Chewing on my bottom lip I consider blurting my question, just to put myself out of my misery. Instead I find myself saying, "I would love that."

"You've got a deal. Can I ask a favor in return?"

He's just offered to take me around the world. Pretty sure whatever he's going to ask is something I'll make sure I can do for him. "Anything."

"I've seen the marketing and promotions for your shop. You have a gift. I was wondering if you'd help me create some for mine?"

A peel of thunder echoes through the forest, growing closer. I smell rain in the air coming in through the windows. "Yes, of course."

He holds out a hand, then remembers the Touch, and withdraws it. I see a new light in his eyes, though. "That's why you didn't want me to touch you yesterday, isn't it? You were afraid you'd see something about my past."

It's not the past I fear. The future is the problem. Another reason I need to remind myself not to fall so hard for this man. I'm not part of that future, if my vision is accurate.

"Like you said, we all have secrets," I remind him. "I never want to invade your privacy, even if it's accidental."

"I get that and appreciate it, but we've shared a kiss, as I recall." A sly grin crosses his face. "Does your gift only work through your hands?"

Gift. I'm sure to many it seems like that. His gaze drops to my lips, and I fight the urge to lick them. He's wondering if I pick up information through other parts of my body. It's kind of cute. "Mostly."

He leans closer, still staring at my mouth. "Mostly?"

Flustered, I chuckle softly. "I pick up things in other ways, too. I am a witch after all."

"Oh yeah? Do you know what I'm about to do right now?"

I hear the patter of rain on the porch. "I don't need psychic abilities to know that," I tease.

When his lips meet mine, my mind goes gloriously blank. Everything in me focuses on the kiss. I forget about Mariel, the kittens, Mrs. Sorensen. I even stop thinking about my sisters and our quest to save Mom. The only thing that exists is Hopper and the strong arms he wraps around he as he pulls me close.

I don't know how long we stay there, leaning into each other. Time ceases to exist, and there's no hurry, no rush to move on to other things.

The fire inside me burns hot and bright. I'm lost in it, and I don't want to stop.

And then through the open window, I hear Cinders squawk. Lightning flashes, and on its heels, thunder booms, as though right above my roof.

It's so loud, it rattles the windows, and both of us jump. The kittens begin to cry and we rush to soothe them.

The storm rages for several minutes. My electricity goes out and I have to light candles. Once the thunder and lightning move on, the rain lingers. It's a gully washer, but the kittens settle enough for Hopper and I to talk and laugh a while longer.

By the light of a candle, I lift the lid on the first box and finger some of it. None would be considered high-end, but I love costume jewelry, and several pieces have genuine stones in them.

With Hopper by my side, I grow bolder. I begin picking up different pieces and placing them in the palm of my hand, waiting for the Touch to kick in.

It doesn't.

I'm somewhat relieved, and I sense Hopper is as well, but I'm also disappointed. Maybe there's no way for me to figure out what happened with Mariel. Or perhaps I can go back to the necklace and try that again.

Usually, things hold a single memory or show me a simple scene from the future. It's not like watching a movie from start to finish, but only getting to see a very small snippet.

I remove the lid from the second and my pulse picks up.

There, in the midst of bracelets and earrings, is the one thing I'm betting will do the trick.

The garnet ring I saw Mariel wearing in my vision.

9

"*G*otcha," I say.

Hopper leans close to have a look. "What is it?"

Using one of the scarves on the arm of the sofa, I pick the ring out and show it to him. "She was wearing this in my vision. Maybe it will give me some information about what happened the night I was shown."

He looks at me solemnly. "You better lay down."

I nod and grab a crystal before making myself comfortable on the area rug, now open because we moved the coffee table closer to the sofa.

"What's that," Hopper asks about the stone.

"Black tourmaline," I tell him. "It repels negativity, and I'm hoping if there's any black magick lingering on this, it'll protect me. I think that's what knocked me on my butt last time. Sometimes I have strong reactions, but it's rare something renders me unconscious."

Lying prone, I close my eyes and hear Hopper moving to kneel beside me. "I'm right here," he says reassuringly.

Feeling his protection is as good as handling the tourmaline. I place the ring on my belly and remove the scarf. Opening my hand, I instruct Hopper to set the ring on it.

The metal feels cool against my skin. A slight buzz tingles my palm. I'm tense waiting for something to happen, and I force myself to take a deep breath and relax my shoulders. Hopper watches me intently, and outside, I hear the last traces of thunder in the distance. Closing my eyes, I turn all my attention to the garnet and ask it to show me Mariel.

A kind of static starts in my ears and my pulse jumps. Mentally, I call out to her spirit and ask it to show me something about her life. Her death.

Seconds tick by and I'm holding my breath again. *Come on*, I think. *Show me something.*

I wait.

And I wait.

Nothing happens.

Out of the four of us, Autumn has the most patience, followed by Spring, then me. Winter has no patience at all. When nothing happens, I imagine Autumn's voice telling me to stop forcing it and relax.

I try again, seeing the ring in my mind's eye. I send energy through my hand to it, imagining warming it, soothing it.

Still, nothing happens, to my great disappointment.

Defeated, I open my eyes to find Hopper staring at me. "Are you getting anything?" he asks.

I shake my head. "I'm sure I saw her wearing this. I thought it would work."

I hold the beautiful ring out so I can look at it, the garnet reflecting almost black in the shadows. Here and there, I see the flicker of candlelight in the stone, energy buzzing like lightning around it.

"Is there anything I can do?" Hopper asks.

I'm about to return the ring to the box when I have an idea. "Let me try one more thing."

I slide it onto my right-hand middle finger. It's a perfect fit. This is how Mariel wore it.

My heart gives a squeeze, a rush of tingling flies up my arm and into my chest. The garnet glows brighter.

The next thing I know, I'm staring at Mariel's hand instead of mine.

I pick up a baby, a little boy whose smile is infectious as he looks at me with dark eyes. His fist swings in the air and I catch it with my lips and give it a kiss. His other hand grasps at my fingers, the ring. His feet kick as I pull him to me, and he makes a noise that sounds like delight.

"We're going to be all right this time," I hear myself as Mariel say. "Your daddy will take care of everything."

I tuck the child into my chest and hug him, the weight of his tiny body melting into mine and reassuring me. Mariel is happy, content, and assured Kaan will protect them. She stares at the ring and it glows.

But underneath her happiness, I feel fear. I taste it on my tongue, along with that metallic flavor from the previous visit. It feels as though the blood in my bones turns sluggish, and that in my heart pumps harder and faster. I'm filled with love for the child and hope for the future, yet, down deep, dread stirs. I understand no matter what Kaan does, I'm doomed. The baby with me.

Two sides of the same coin. Utter happiness and sheer sorrow at what is to come. It seems to rip her heart in two.

That pain sends me back to the present, where I gasp, and Hopper helps me sit up as I struggle to tug the ring off.

He holds onto my shoulders. "What did you see?"

"Mariel and one of her babies." My throat hurts trying to speak. I set the ring on the coffee table and rub my hands together, a sudden coldness flooding me. "She was afraid for the baby, and herself, I think. But she wanted to believe Kaan would save them both."

"From what?"

I shake my head, unsure, thoughts and feelings clouding my system as I try to weed Mariel's from mine. "She definitely felt as though something was coming for them. Something awful." I'm nearly in tears, wishing I could return and protect them. I rub the spot on my chest where I swear I can still feel the baby resting. "Oh Hopper, what happened to them?"

He pulls me gently into an embrace, rubbing my back and allowing me to shed the tears. It grows darker outside, even though the thunder and lightning have moved off. The temperature has dropped considerably and I shiver.

After a few moments, we break our embrace and he asks if he can get me something to eat or drink. I shake my head, and hang onto one of his hands, allowing myself to feel secure and grounded in his presence.

He stares into my eyes and I know he wants to kiss me again. I want that, too. At the moment, I want it more than anything.

But there's something I have to know first. Before I let this go any farther.

"I was holding that baby," I tell him. "It felt good, right."

He runs his thumb over my knuckles, a soft caressing gesture. "I bet you'll make a good mom someday."

"I'm not having children."

He seems to take this with no surprise. "Okay."

That's it? "Do you want to have kids?"

He shrugs.

A non-answer. What does that mean? I stand and go to the small fireplace on the other side. I fiddle with a couple of the sticks, using my body to block Hopper's view. I simply hold out my hands and start a small fire. "You don't talk much about your family or growing up."

I hear him shift and glance over my shoulder. He looks away. "Not a lot worth discussing."

"What about marriage and family for you? Have you thought about it?"

His focus returns to my face, questioning. "Where is this coming from?"

Fair enough, I'm fishing. Not for the reason he thinks, though.

I return to sit next to him. "I have to be honest. If you have any desire to have children"—the leftover emotions from Mariel are making me bold—"then you don't want to start a relationship with me. I'm serious when I say I'm not having any."

He gives me a funny look. We've shared a couple kisses, and here I am talking about having kids with him. "Fine. You don't have to." He leans forward with a smile. "And you're not getting rid of me that easily."

A tiny spark of relief flares to life in my belly. "You don't want to know why?"

He shrugs again. "None of my business, but I assume you have a good reason, and that's good enough for me."

I wait for more, but he doesn't say anything else. He just keeps smiling at me.

The rain eases and my lights return. I study his face carefully in the stronger illumination and still find no pretense. It's too good to be true.

This closeness, this vulnerability, makes me antsy. If I don't do something to distract myself, I'll jump his bones. "I think I'll have some tea now," I say, rising to my feet.

He helps me stand, then follows me to the kitchen. "Got anything stronger?"

I rummage in my pantry and pull out a bottle of blackberry wine. "If you like this, you can have the whole thing. Spring started making it last year, but it's too sweet and heavy for me."

He eyes the bottle skeptically. "Maybe I'll just have tea, too."

As I prepare two cups, I give him more details about what I saw and felt. "I'm confused about Mariel and Kaan. In the first vision, I felt sick when he gave Mariel the necklace and she knew it was loaded with black magick. Kaan didn't appear in this vision, and I don't know who gave her the ring, but she seemed to believe he would keep her and the baby safe. That's at odds with what I was picking up from her before. *And* him."

Hopper takes a seat on one of my stools at the breakfast bar. "Any hint of black magick this time with the ring?"

"None. That's part of why I'm confused."

"So we're at a dead end?"

"I wonder if I could get anything else from the necklace," I say as much to myself as him.

"Do you want to try on any of the other stuff?"

"Maybe."

I feel Autumn's energy before she knocks. "Come on in, sister," I call out.

Hopper turns toward the front door. "Your sister is here?"

My living room and kitchen are one big room and I see Autumn inch the door open. Her smile turns knowing when she sees Hopper. "Just wanted to check on you. Did you lose power?"

"For a few minutes. Would you like a cup of tea?"

Sirius, her dog familiar, noses his way in and makes a beeline for the kittens. He sniffs at them carefully and looks up at her.

She pats his head and he sits. "We won't stay." She sees the ring on the coffee table. "Did you get another hit on that woman?"

Although it's still drizzling, she's completely dry. I'm sure she used a spell to umbrella her and her familiar. In her hand, I notice a wrapped package.

"Yes, but it's not helpful in figuring things out about her death."

"If her husband was into black magick, maybe we don't want to know more. We have enough on our plates without stirring that up."

Winter is the oldest but Autumn acts like our mother most of the time. Responsible, dependable, and always trying to keep the four of us out of trouble.

Seems like it finds us anyway.

"Kaan Fontaine is definitely a bad dude," I tell her. "Who knows what he did to Mariel, and maybe to other women as well? If he's killing people, we have to stop him."

She looks at me with dark eyes, so much like Dad's. "We can't save everyone, Summer."

Watch me. It's a knee jerk comeback. She's right, but I wish I *could.* "I know."

She brings the package over and sets it on the counter. "Dad dropped this off for you today."

A tiny bird of panic flutters in my chest. "He's not going to miss my birthday, is he? He promised to be here."

"He will. He said you need this now."

Hopper lifts his cup. "It's your birthday?"

"On the twentieth, which is also summer solstice this year."

69

"The longest day in the Northern Hemisphere." He takes a sip and sets the cup down. "Pretty cool to have it on that day."

It *is* like a cool gift since I love the sun.

"She's a Gemini, cusp Cancer," Autumn tells him. "Her rising sign is Leo—that's why she likes being in the spotlight. Moon in Sagittarius—she longs for travel."

Hopper nods, acting as though he followed all of that, but I can see in his eyes he's not quite sure what she's talking about.

"Autumn is an astrology expert." I grab the gift, admiring my father's handiwork at turning pressed leaves into paper. There are hand drawn pictures of phoenixes, and I smile at his ingenuity. "She looks at people's birth charts and can tell a lot about them from where the planets and stars were aligned that day."

"Fascinating," he says, eyeing the package. "I think I'm a Pisces, but I'm not sure."

"Come see me," Autumn says. "I'll need your date of birth, time, and where you were born. I might be able to shed some insight into your personality, emotional triggers, and other fun stuff, like karmic challenges."

"She can even tell you things about your past lives," I tell him as I begin to carefully unwrap the paper. I don't want to wreck the pictures my father has drawn.

"That might be more information than I need," Hopper jokes.

There's a box under the paper, and I lift the lid. My breath catches as I see a beautiful metal phoenix pendant on a chain. The eyes are a bright gold, the color of citrine. "It's beautiful."

I hold it up for the others to see, and there's something

in Hopper's face that alerts me he's already seen it. Power ebbs and flows from the pendant as I turn it in the light.

"Wow," Autumn says, winking at Hopper. "That's stunning."

A thought dawns on me. "Did you make this?"

He comes to my side of the breakfast bar and wiggles his fingers at the necklace, offering to put it on me. "I might have had a hand in it. Or a small blowtorch, in this case."

The metal warms instantly on my skin. I reach up to touch the tiny bird, feeling as if it's belonged to me all along. My father's power radiates from it.

"We made sure to clear it's energy before Dad wrapped it," Autumn says.

All I feel coming from it is our father's love and protection. "It's amazing. I love it."

"Figured you would," my sister says. "Dad always knows the right gift at the right time, doesn't he?"

It's true. He's a shaman and has his own unique set of skills and psychic abilities. I wish we saw him more, but he's the leader of a small tribe of outcasts and they need him as much as his daughters do.

Autumn and Sirius head for the door. I follow in order to see them out.

"I can take the kittens," she says softly under her breath, "if you need a little... privacy tonight."

I glance back at Hopper, who is helping himself to a glass from my cupboard. He looks so at home here.

"I don't think that'll be necessary," I tell my nosey sister. "But I'll keep it in mind for future opportunities."

She hugs me, laughing softly. "It's your birthday, Summer. Maybe it's time you give yourself a gift."

As I close the door behind her, I consider taking her

71

words to heart. Back at the breakfast bar, Hopper tastes the wine and makes a face.

"I warned you," I say.

He laughs. "Why didn't you tell me about your birthday?"

I finger the pendant, feeling my father's protective energies flying around me. "It appears you're already in the know."

"Your dad asked if I could make something for him. I had no idea it'd be something as tiny as a piece of jewelry, but I'm always up for a challenge. He didn't tell me it was a birthday gift. I was supposed to have another day or two to work on it, but he showed up at my shop last night, insisting I finish it right away. He said you needed it."

Winter probably talked to Dad and told him about Kaan and the black magick. Either that, or he was on one of his shamanic quests and saw I needed extra protection. "He's an awesome father in many ways."

Hopper goes back to his tea, but I can tell it doesn't taste right after the lingering flavor of the wine. "He doesn't say much, does he?"

If he only knew. I laugh and sit down to tell Hopper a few more stories about my family.

10

The next morning, I wake to find five small bodies nestled against me in my bed. After Hopper left, they only woke once before dawn to be fed and went back to sleep with ease. It was hard to say good-bye to Hopper but having the kittens helped. As I prepared for bed, I couldn't decide whether to be happy or contrite with myself. He and I are so good together, but I still feel like I might be misleading him.

Destiny is a funny thing. If he was supposed to end up with the woman in my vision, creating a family with her, was he still "available" to have a fling with me?

Bringing the kittens, I leave my cabin, after feeding Cinders and making my morning offering to Hestia. I say an extra prayer to my mom asking for her guidance with my new relationship. Even if Hopper is the man for me, I must brace myself for heartbreak, from the vision I had at Beltane.

The morning is clear after the storms, the smell of pine trees surrounding my cabin strong. The path winding past my sisters' cabins to Conjure is covered with branches and flowers strewn across it from last night's winds. While the sun is warm, everything is still wet.

Inside the shop's kitchen, I find my sisters sharing cups of tea and coffee, along with fresh muffins from the oven. They look at me over the edges of their cups with sly smiles as they greet the kittens.

"Long night?" Spring asks with a grin. She hands me a glass of lavender lemonade—one of my favorites.

I accept it and enjoy the iced liquid as it goes down my throat. She's added a smidge of honey, gathered from our new beehives, and it tastes extra delicious. "Why do you ask?"

Winter scratches Vivaldi's head. "What time did Hopper leave?"

I give her my most innocent look. "Around midnight, why?"

Spring and Autumn giggle, sounding like girls. I glance between all three. "What?"

I know what they're hinting at, but I refuse to play along.

"It's good to see the two of you together," Autumn says. "He makes you happy."

He does that. "Don't read too much into it. He's helping with the kittens, that's all."

Spring chuckles. "Have you done their birth charts to see if they're compatible, Autumn?"

She puts a finger to her lips as if she's in on the joke and has already checked them. "It's pretty clear they're a good match."

Winter rolls her eyes. "Hopper's doing more than helping you with the kittens, and you can quit pretending we don't know."

"I really shouldn't get involved with him."

Autumn *tsks*. "Why not? You're still hung up on that vision, aren't you?"

At the beginning of the summer, I had a lot of hope for the coming season and my relationship with Hopper. But the night at the Beltane celebration, everything changed.

He was about the age he is now, and the mere fact he appeared unaged makes me believe his impending marriage will be sooner rather than later.

And there's nothing I can do about it.

At least beyond what I've thought about. Confession number three—I'm a charm caster.

I've considered casting three different charms on him. Messing with fate is dangerous territory, and so far, I've resisted doing anything more than putting protection spells on him.

Winter sees the sad look on my face and grabs my arm. "Have you had another?"

I shake my head.

Autumn picks up Beethoven and cuddles him close, her features worried as she glances at me. "Not even when he kissed you?"

"How do you know...?" I leave the sentence hanging because *duh*, there's not much I can keep from my sisters. Of course, they know, but I eye Winter suspiciously anyway. "You weren't sneaking around my cabin last night, were you?"

One of her strongest abilities is her invisibility spells. She's a master at it, and I suspect she uses it more than the rest of us know. Not because she's nosey, per se, but she believes it's her duty to protect our family. She also doesn't like us to know how much she worries, so she uses her magick to check on us. It's sort of her way of being our mother now.

She grins, but not because I've caught her. "None of us need to be psychic, nor do I need to sneak around and catch you and Hopper in the act, to see how much you're in love with him."

"And him with you," Spring adds.

"I'm not in love with Hopper Caldwell," I argue, even though it's a lie, something I never do to my sisters because I have no reason to. Of course, they'll know, but it goes deeper than that. So, it surprises me when I don't tell them the truth, but my relationship with Hopper feels too new, too fragile. I want to keep it all to myself a while longer.

Winter snorts derisively. "Oh please. Enjoy it, Summer. You deserve happiness."

It's not that simple. "Do you think my vision about him might be wrong now? That something has changed in the timeline and he won't marry someone else?"

"If you haven't received any more hits about it," Autumn says, "it could be because it *has* changed. You shouldn't hold back because of one vision. Like Winter said, enjoy what you have with him right now. Trying to control what might happen in the future is out of our hands."

Harm none. I look at my feet and shuffle them a bit. "I know, but there's also the fact that even if he's not going to die anytime soon, if he does want a serious relationship— love, marriage, and kids—I'm not the girl for him."

"Wow, you *are* serious," Winter exclaims with a smile. "You also worry too much."

"Look who's calling the cauldron black," I say, but return the smile, so she knows I'm joking.

"I'm the oldest, it's my job."

No joking there. My turn to roll my eyes. "We all deserve happiness, Winter."

The phone rings and Spring goes out front to answer it. I

dig into a muffin and watch Winter feed the kittens, my brain turning things over and over.

"That was Mrs. Sorensen," Spring says when she comes back. "She wants to know if you and your 'handsome friend' can bring spring water again this week. She said the last dose revived her quite a bit."

I swallow the last bite and nod. "Did she have a day in mind? My schedule is packed today."

"She said to make it at your convenience. She's so nice."

"Is there anything we can help you with to free up your schedule?" Autumn asks.

"I can handle the blog," Winter volunteers.

Autumn nods. "I can take your energy clients."

She's a Reiki Master and well versed in the chakra system. "That'd be very helpful. I'll call my clients and let them know you'll be handling them. Thanks."

"Do you think Hopper can help with the water?" Spring asks with a wink. "Seems like his visit helped Mrs. Sorensen feel better as well."

I can't keep the grin off my face. "Guess we'll find out."

Spring reaches out to finger my new necklace from Dad. "This turned out beautifully."

I slept with it on last night, and I'm sure that, along with the kittens and residual energy from Hopper, helped me sleep deeper than I have in days. "Absolutely. I feel like Dad is with me all the time now."

"Have you decided on a theme?" Autumn asks.

Normally, they throw a small party for me, inviting a bunch of my friends. Last year, we did a mermaid theme. The year before that was the sixties, the four of us dressing like the Beatles.

The parties are totally a blast, but this year, the day feels different as I approach twenty-five. I actually thought I'd be happily married by now and traveling the world with my husband. Life had other plans.

But I'm not unhappy living here with the three of them and running the shop. I see by their faces they want to have a party because we always have so much fun. Since Mom's death last fall, fun hasn't been on our agendas much. "How about a fairy theme? Summer solstice is a high holiday for them."

Spring squeals, Autumn smiles, and Winter nods approval.

"This is going to be so fun!" Spring does a little dance. "We'll string lights in the garden, have a fortune teller, play tambourines and banjoes. I'll get Hale and Storm to help."

Hale is our shop handyman, and Storm is Spring's best friend. The two finally got together at Beltane, and they've been inseparable since.

Autumn returns Beethoven to the box and picks up Chopin. "I'll start sending invites."

"You know, I bet Hale can find us an old wagon to decorate," Winter says.

Hale has the ability to either build or find whatever we need, whenever we need it. That's its own kind of magick, in my book.

"What kind of food should we have?" Spring goes behind her counter and starts opening recipe books.

I'm thinking about food, fairy wings, and how I'm going to braid my hair, when suddenly my vision of Beltane imposes itself over the kitchen around us. I want to be happy, but I see Hopper with his son, pushing him in the swing and smiling at the woman whose face I can't see.

It's hard to look forward to my birthday with that weighing down my heart.

*a*s if I've brought it on myself, the vision grows stronger, shifting. It's not the one from Beltane anymore. This is fresh, showing me Hopper, lying on the floor of his shop, eyes vacant. My skin prickles with icicles. Black magick.

"No!" I scream.

As if in a vacuum, I hear someone call my name. "Summer!"

Winter is shaking me. "It's okay. We're here."

I come out of it with a jerk, my head spinning, my words tripping over themselves. "Hopper...black magick...wizard..."

My sisters help me into a chair. Spring brings a bottle of orange and frankincense and waves the oils under my nose.

The biting scent clears my brain fog. Autumn hands me my cup of tea and insists I drink. I accept it, but my hands shake so bad, some of the liquid slips over the edge and spills on me. She takes the cup and sets it back on the table as Winter kneels in front of me.

"Deep breath, sister. Tell us what you saw."

The kittens mewl frantically from the commotion. My head continues to swim, and I blink, focusing on the table. "I need to get to Hopper. Fontaine—I think he's at the shop —I couldn't tell. But I know Hopper's in danger—Fontaine's going to kill him."

My sisters exchange glances and Winter rises, pulling me up with her. "I'll take her."

Autumn nods. "I'm coming, too."

"I'll have to stay, take care of the shop and kittens," Spring says. "If you need me, call."

My older two sisters hustle me to the parking lot where we jump into Winter's VW Bug. "Hurry," I say, pulse racing.

What if we're too late?

We tear out and head north on the highway, flying past slower vehicles, as Autumn and Winter discuss how to handle the dark wizard if he's still there.

"We should've brought Spring." I worry my necklace. "She could have frozen him and then we could..."

I don't say it, but I know my sisters read my mind. It's wrong to take someone's life, but at this moment I'm prepared to do it if it means saving Hopper.

"I can cloak us so he can't see us," Winter says. "What do you think, Autumn?"

"Cloak Summer. I can't use telekinesis or astral travel if I'm invisible. We might need both."

It seems too far, the few miles to Hopper's shop. It feels like a lifetime.

We pull in, tires screaming and kicking up rocks. The shop is dark, no cars out front. He doesn't open until eleven most days, so that shouldn't be a surprise, and yet I worry that somehow, he opened early and the black magick has already killed him.

I rush to the front door and notice the closed sign. I bang

on the frame with my fist, "Hopper! Hopper, are you in there?"

When I get no answer, I cup my hands around my eyes to peer into the glass, my focus going to the place where I saw his body in the vision.

It's not there.

For a heartbeat, I feel relief, but what if Fontaine simply moved him?

Winter and Autumn come up behind me. "Is he in there?" Winter asks.

"I can't see him." I bang again and yell for him. "Please, don't let us be too late," I pray to Hestia, and any other god or goddess who might be listening.

Autumn and Winter fan out, looking through the large windows on either side.

"I'm going around back," I tell them.

I take off, nearly twisting my ankle in the rocks. There's a long drive along the side of the house that leads to the rear, and I see Hopper's truck, along with his moving van.

I run up the stairs to the porch and repeat my banging and calling on the back door. I see no signs of the wizard, feel no black magick prickling my skin, but I'm still in such a state I'm practically sobbing.

Jiggling the door handle, I find it open, nearly falling into Hopper's kitchen. His store is laid out much like ours, the shop in the front with living quarters in the back. He also has an upstairs, which I assume contains his bed and bath.

The coffee maker is on a timer and starts to brew as I blow through the kitchen, past a side room and toward the front. I unlock it and let my sisters in. "I can't find him."

Sunlight spills through the plate glass windows, illuminating most of the shop. Frantically, I scan in all directions, behind bureaus, over the top of a large sofa.

Winter and Autumn do the same. I can tell by Winter's body language there is a spirit here, maybe more than one, attached to some of the items. She works hard to ignore them.

I start to run back to the kitchen, the smell of brewing coffee filtering through the rooms, but pause a moment in the doorway. Hopper stood here in my vision looking at the person who came through the door. It had to be Fontaine.

I work to conjure the vision once more, hoping to see the man's face. I concentrate, tuning out my sisters.

I get nothing, not even a hint of black magick.

My phoenix heats against my skin so hot it nearly burns. I feel a presence behind me, and I whirl, throwing my hands out ready to go on the defense.

"Summer?"

I'm looking at an alive Hopper, whose wet hair is combed back from his face. The scent of his soap and shampoo washes over me.

Reality hits so hard my knees go weak. I start to drop and he reaches out to grab me. "What's wrong?"

The sound of his baritone voice brings up a fresh sob and I fall into his chest, gripping his shirt in both hands. "Oh, thank the goddess. You're okay."

I sense his confusion as one arm wraps around me. "Of course, I am. What's going on?"

I hesitate, drawing back and wondering if I should divulge what I saw. How can I? Then I might have to explain the Beltane vision and how I can see the future at times. That's definitely not a discussion I want to have at the moment. You don't just tell someone you've seen their death.

Winter comes to my rescue. "We came by to invite you to Summer's birthday party."

"Yes," Autumn jumps in, "Sunday at five o'clock. We're doing a fairy theme. We were hoping you might come early and help us set up."

I love my sisters. They understand the tough position I'm in right now. Do I have a responsibility to tell someone about their impending death, even though I don't know specific details such as the date or exactly what happens to them? Or is warning a person just messing with fire? If it's fate to be done with this life and move onto the next stage and I create bad karma, am I creating it for myself trying to stop that from happening?

Times like this, I want to give fate the middle finger. Unfortunately, I can't protect Hopper twenty-four hours a day, even with my charms. Warning him could bring undue stress and the exact thing I don't want to happen.

When I was eight, I tried to warn a friend about an accident I saw happen to her. We were just kids and I didn't realize that everyone didn't have my gift. I was at her house playing and we took turns riding her bike.

The Touch showed her on her bike in a future time wearing her favorite yellow shirt. She was riding on the sidewalk, but a truck left the road and struck her.

You can imagine her reaction when I told her what I'd seen. She ran into her house bawling, then her mother came out a minute later to yell at me. It wasn't long after that my mom picked me up and the woman yelled at her as well.

But that experience struck a chord, and rather than testing fate, her parents put the girl's bike in the garage. My friend was not allowed to ride it, then two weeks later, her cousin was visiting, got bored and found it in the garage. She pulled it out and went for a ride.

At lunch, she'd spilled spaghetti on her shirt and my friend's mother had made her change, so she was wearing the yellow shirt when she hopped on the bike and rode it down to the end of the block. On her way back, she was struck by a truck, her body thrown, receiving multiple broken bones.

Even though I told them, I couldn't stop what happened. It taught me a valuable lesson—trying to prevent certain accidents or situations was in fact, destiny creating the right situation for the thing I was trying to prevent. Sometimes, there is no escaping fate, no matter how hard we try. Just because you can see the future doesn't mean you can save the ones you love.

Harm none. Predicting the future could actually do harm, right?

Hopper touches my face, a frown creasing his forehead. The tone of his voice doesn't match the words when he says, "Yeah, I'd be happy to come early and help. Sounds awesome. Are you sure you're okay? I mean, you could've just called."

I laugh, simply to relieve the pressure inside my chest and pat him gently on the arm. "We had to make a run this way anyhow," I stumble over my words, "and I was hoping you could hang out at the shop today. Watch the kittens for me... Oh, and I need to take more water to Mrs. Sorensen."

I'm trying to find any reason to keep him close so I can protect him, regardless of what the vision has shown me. "If you can spend another day with me, I could use the help."

Consternation flitters over his face as he looks around. He's already been closed the last two days for the most part, thanks to me. Doing so again is not good for business. "I can take an hour or so, then bring the kittens here."

There's not a lot I can do to convince him otherwise. The biggest thing is to get him away from here for now. If Fontaine comes by and sees the shop closed, maybe he won't return. Or I can figure out another way to keep Hopper busy and out of the dark wizard's grasp.

"Perfect," I say even though it's not. "Do you want to come with us right now?"

Hopper gives me another questioning look, but he seems to pick up on my anxiety and runs his hands up and down my arms in a reassuring gesture. "Give me five minutes."

He turns and goes into his kitchen, then I hear him jog up the stairs. I look at my sisters and they embrace me. They look as relieved as I am we found him alive and he's leaving with us.

"I'm not sure how to keep him away from this place," I murmur.

"Don't worry," Autumn says. "We'll figure something out."

Winter glances around, her eyes landing on certain pieces of furniture. I'm sure the spirits are talking to her because she offers a soft, "not now," before she turns to me. "We'll keep him busy all day and figure something out for later."

Hopper returns and takes a sheet of paper from behind the counter, using a marker to write a message on it. *Be back this afternoon*, it says. *Call and leave a message if you need something.* He adds his cell number.

He tapes it to the window on the front door. "Let me grab some coffee. I probably should take my truck, too, in order to haul the water."

If he doesn't have his vehicle, he's more likely to rely on us for a ride. "Oh no, we'll take the shop van," I tell him. "No sense burning all your gas."

Another odd look, then he shrugs, disappearing once more. The three of us are about to go out to Winter's car when I feel that prickling sensation hit. Just as Autumn opens the door, I yell, "No!"

But it's too late.

Standing in front of us is Kaan Fontaine.

12

*A*utumn slams the door and locks it.

Winter murmurs a quick spell, turning herself invisible. "Meet me out back," her disembodied voice says.

I sense her moving away, and she sends a picture to my mind's eye, showing her driving the car there and picking us up.

I throw a charm on it and the windows, blocking Fontaine's view. Autumn grabs my hand and we run to the kitchen. Hopper glances at us, startled as he's putting the lid on his travel mug.

"Gotta go." I grab his arm and jerk him behind us.

I hear the rumble of the VW's motor starting. Autumn mumbles a spell under her breath as we get to the back door, sending extra protection over all of us.

The Phoenix flares hot again, and I tap into it, asking it to add its protection to ours and to aid Winter's speed.

We're outside and Hopper is locking up when the VW swings into view.

"Hurry," I say to him and he gives me another of those *what is wrong with you* looks before finishing with his keys.

Before he can pocket them, I force him down the back stairs to the car.

"What's the hurry?" he asks.

I practically throw him into the back seat before diving in myself.

Winter does a quick U-turn in the small rear lot, and we peel off toward the front. Just as we're about to clear the shop, ten yards from the highway, Kaan steps into our path.

We all gasp, and Hopper asks "Hey, isn't that the guy from yesterday?"

"Do not stop," I command Winter.

She yanks the wheel right to avoid the dark wizard, but it's as if he knows she's going to do that, and he suddenly appears in front of us a second time.

Magick.

Winter jerks left. Fontaine follows, appearing yet again.

"Run him down," I say between gritted teeth.

"It's a projection," Autumn states. She's a master at sending her astral self to other places, so she knows. "It's not really him."

"Alrighty then," Winter says. She angles the car toward the highway once more, nearly giving me whiplash with the acceleration.

I pray she's right, even though part of me doesn't care if it's truly him, or his astral self.

"I don't think this is a good idea," Hopper chimes in, rearing back in the seat.

Everyone braces as we mow down the last couple feet, waiting for impact. I keep one hand on Hopper, the other on the door handle, and anticipate the hit I know is coming.

We pass right through him. Only when I hear Winter cackle loudly and the car reaches the highway do I relax my grip.

A glance behind us shows Kaan still at the shop. His dark eyes follow the car as we head south to Conjure. He doesn't move, simply stands there watching.

I slouch down, placing a hand over my heart. It's racing so hard, I feel like I'm lightheaded.

"Do I want to know what just happened?" Hopper asks.

"No," all three of us answer at the same time.

He's quiet a moment, his big body folded like an accordion in the small back seat. Eventually, curiosity gets the best of him. "That guy was right in front of the car. Several times. How did he move that fast? How did we not *hit* him?"

I glance over and meet his eyes. I see realization kicking in.

"Ohhh, got it. Black magick dude." He runs a hand over his face and into his hair. "That's why you showed up, isn't it? You knew he was coming. He's figured out who I am."

I don't see any point in going into details. "He means you harm, I'm sure of it. You need to stick with us. We can keep you safe."

Hopper glances out his window, digesting this information. "You can't protect me for the rest of my life, Summer. Whatever the guy wants, I'll have to handle him."

Winter meets my eyes in the rearview mirror, her mouth a thin line. I'm not sure if she thinks I should tell Hopper the truth or not. For now, I'm relieved he's here and alive. We'll figure out what to tell him once we're at Conjure.

We fly down the highway in silence. I keep checking to make sure Fontaine hasn't followed. I see no sign of him, but I'm paranoid enough that it'll be hard not to keep looking over my shoulder for a while.

Right before we reach the turn off for our shop, Hopper grabs my hand. I slide my eyes from the road to look at him and see the strength in his face. The determination. His attention drops to my phoenix necklace. "The eyes are glow-ing," he says.

Looking down, I raise the pendant, seeing what he sees. They are indeed bright, and I feel my father's energy growing stronger.

When we reach our property, we find Don "Big Eagle" Whitethorne waiting for us.

13

My father is a mix of Creek and Irish, but his Native American features are prominent. His long gray hair is braided down his back, his skin a ruddy color. He wears a short sleeve button down shirt with a black vest embroidered with beads in a flying eagle pattern over it. His jeans are adorned with a silver eagle belt buckle. His leather boots are black and worn but clean.

He embraces each of his daughters, holding onto me a couple extra seconds. "Thank you for the gift," I tell him. "It's beautiful."

He glances at Hopper before returning his attention to me. "Do not take it off. You need it."

I introduce Hopper to him, forgetting after all the excitement that they already know each other.

"Yes, we've met." Dad extends a hand to Hopper and they shake. "Thank you for taking care of my daughter."

Hopper nods. "My pleasure, although to be honest, I think she's protected me more than I have her."

"We have a situation," Winter tells Dad and he doesn't

seem surprised. "Could Autumn and I speak to you in private?"

Spring is out front with the kittens. As Winter and Autumn take Dad to my treatment room, I rub my forehead and try not to collapse into a chair. I'm not all that worried about Fontaine coming here. If he knows who we are and what we do, he'll stay away from us. But I must decide how far I'm willing to go to figure out what happened to his wife.

"Can I get you some breakfast?" I ask Hopper, as if it's just another day in the neighborhood. He likes Spring's scones, so I expect him to ask for one of those.

Instead, he shakes his head. "Are you going to explain what's going on?"

I bite the inside of my bottom lip. "Is it okay if I don't?"

A touch of exasperation enters his expression as he takes a seat. "I can handle it, Summer."

The question is, can I? "I'll be right back."

I jump up and dash to get a scone. Spring finishes with a customer and slides behind the counter. Consternation is written all over her face. "What happened?" she asks under her breath.

The two customers in the shop pay no attention to us, engrossed in a conversation about tarot cards as they suggest different decks to each other from our collection. I give Spring a quick rundown and watch as her eyes grow wide with shock.

"Holy goddess, what are you going to do?"

"I have to tell Hopper at least part of the truth about my visions, I think. The biggest problem is keeping him safe. I can't let him go back to the antique store."

She picks up a pen and sticks it in the cup holder next to the cash register. "Have you put a protection charm on him?"

I fiddle with a clean plate, placing a couple scones on it. "Yes, but it might not be strong enough. Autumn had Sirius bring me Mom's book of spells,"—Sirius is the keeper of this very magickal, very important family heirloom—"but it doesn't cover black magick, even though she was..." I stop myself. My sisters don't know that I saw her toying with it in the mirror. I strongly suspect it contributed to her death.

Spring straightens, giving me a curious stare and I force my mind to go blank so she can't read it. She gathers the rest of the baked goods under the glass cover, seemingly ignorant about any wrongdoing Mom might've engaged in. "Did you charm Hopper's store? I mean did this Fontaine fellow actually get inside?"

Thank the goddess she dropped the black magick discussion. "Come to think of it, no. We never gave him the chance, but I suppose he could have projected inside if he wanted to. He was certainly adept at it."

"Maybe your charm was working."

She could be right. "So, I need to cast a spell over the entire land Hopper owns."

Spring nods, looking speculative. "It certainly couldn't hurt, and I can help you. With my earth magick, we can make sure he can't step foot anywhere close to the antique store."

"Then all I have to do is keep him safe every time he leaves his land. Piece of cake, right?" I tell her sarcastically.

My tone brings a smile to her face. "We'll figure it out," she says, putting a hand on my arm. I groan at how many times I've heard that today

"We have to," I agree. "This is my fault, Spring. I brought this on him."

She squeezes my arm. There's really nothing she can say,

knowing in truth I *am* the one who put Hopper in Fontaine's sights.

When I return to the kitchen, Hopper is staring at his travel mug. His mind seems a thousand miles away and he barely acknowledges when I slide a scone in front of him. "Thanks."

I resume my seat across from him. "I don't like to talk about my gifts. Not to anyone but my sisters and my father."

He glances up, startled at my conversation, but then he nods and looks down again. "I get that, but you already told me about the one. Obviously, you weren't touching me this morning when you saw something, and I'm assuming it has to do with Fontaine showing up at my place."

"I possess claircognizance."

His bushy eyebrows rise. "You can see the future?"

"Yes and no," I admit. "Each of my sisters has varying degrees of the Sight—that's what we call it. In my case, I have no control over what I see or when. Sometimes it works in conjunction with the Touch, or as you saw with Mariel's jewelry, I receive a vision of the past. I don't always know which, but this morning, I had one that seemed to involve Kaan coming into your shop and meaning you harm."

His pause is weighted. "It must have been pretty serious from the way you barged in screaming at the top of your lungs."

"I'm so sorry about invading your privacy. I was more concerned about your health."

"I appreciate that, I think." He fidgets with his travel mug. "And now, you don't want me to go back because you think he'll be waiting for me, or show up again?"

"I actually do need help with the water, and well... Oh,

Hopper, this is all my fault! If I hadn't gone to Fontaine's and been nosey, none of this would be happening."

"It was my idea. You didn't know the guy was into black magick."

"Maybe it'd be better if I dropped the whole thing regarding Mariel. I feel like I'm letting her down, but I can't risk your..." I stop myself before I say *life*. "My main concern right now is keeping you safe."

"Well, unless you're going to move in with me, I'm not sure how you can watch me twenty-four-seven. Wouldn't it be better to teach me how to defend myself against this jerk? Is there a spell or something I can learn?"

He seems completely at ease talking about all this, while I'm freaking out. How ironic. "He has significant magickal powers, Hopper." *And you're not a witch.*

He leans forward, pinning me with his beautiful eyes. "What you're saying is I don't stand a chance against him."

"I know you have skills, but fists and weapons won't work to overpower him."

He sets his jaw, frustrated. With a sigh, he sits back, sips his coffee, and looks at me. "I refuse to live in fear. He's flesh and blood, magick or not, and that means he's mortal like the rest of us."

Mortal. Something in the back of my mind waves a flag to get my attention.

"Holy magick! What if he's not?"

"What?"

"What if Mariel is an immortal?"

Hopper looks completely confused at my sudden left turn. "What are you talking about? She died last week."

Did she? "I wonder how many times she's lived and died."

His eyes narrowed. "You lost me."

Dark magick deals with raising the dead.

"Let's take care of Mrs. Sorensen," I say, rising. "I need to think on this."

14

$\mathcal{A}$t the hot spring, we fill the buckets in silence.

"So, what else can you do?" Hopper finally asks. "You know, with magick?"

We've come too far to pretend I don't know what he's talking about. "My element is fire. I can heat water, start fires, that sort of thing."

"Seriously?" He gives me a grin. "How flippin' cool is that?"

I love that there is no doubt on his face about me or magick. "Want to see?"

He sets down his bucket and puts his hands on his hips. "Of course."

Nearby are the remains of two cabins. From what we know, there were originally twelve families that inhabited this area in the late 1600s before everyone disappeared. My sisters and I own the only four still standing.

I walk to the nearest ruin, a few timbers and stones outlining the original foundation, and hold out both hands toward a pile of brush.

Within seconds, the twigs begin to smolder, a thin line of vapor rising.

"Holy smokes," Hopper says. "Literally."

I laugh and it feels good as the twigs burst into flames. We watch as the colors of red, orange, and yellow light up as the flames grow higher.

The rains last night soaked nature pretty well, but the midday sun is drying things out. I don't want to set the area on fire, or the woods, so I pick up a bucket, scoop up some water, and return.

I watch the beautiful flames for another moment before I douse them. I love the smell of burning wood, and I watch the thin smoke to see which way it rises.

It flows slightly toward me, meaning my wish and spells are favorable, but it also goes slightly right—I need to use my head and not my heart in this situation.

Hopper is still smiling, and his eyes are filled with fascination. "That was amazing."

Turning my face to the sun I smile, too. "I try to focus on my healing gifts, rather than my destructive ones, but I have to say, there's a lot of power in the latter. Fire burns away what no longer serves and that allows what needs to grow fresh and new."

We finish up. Before we leave, I have Spring see if she can pick up Fontaine's energy in the area. She can't and we leave, removing the magnetic signs from the side of the shop van just in case.

At Mrs. Sorensen's estate, we unload before knocking.

I'm surprised when she answers herself. She's looking much better, although her hands shake as she motions us in with a smile. "I'm so glad you could come," she says.

"Are you feeling better?" I ask.

"Much. I even gave Linda the day off. She's been working

a lot of overtime while I was sick, and I thought she needed rest."

Hopefully, her daughter doesn't show up. We chat a few more minutes as Hopper brings the water in and dumps it in the tub. As Mrs. Sorensen and I walk the hallway, I ask a question that's been bugging me. "Did you happen to know Mariel Fontaine? Your neighbor a couple houses north of here?"

She looks slightly startled, glancing to the left as we move out of Hopper's way. "Yes, she was a good friend of mine. I was shocked about her death. A terrible loss."

"She wasn't sick or anything before she passed?"

"She was having a few bad days, but always seemed in good health. Her poor husband is lost without her. Apparently, she was just sitting in a chair reading when her heart stopped."

The memory of that open book flashes across my mind. "You know her husband, too?"

We enter the bathroom and I remove the bracelets from my wrist so I can put my hands in the water to warm it.

"I don't know Kaan as well as I did Mariel, but yes."

Hesitancy in her voice makes me look at her. "You don't like him, do you?"

Her eyes slide away from mine again and she fiddles with the hem of her shirt, pulling off an invisible thread. "He tends to keep to himself. I do know he was completely devoted to Mariel. Her happiness and well-being always came first."

The hot spring water is soft and caressing underneath my hands as I send heat into it. "What will he do now that she's gone?"

"I don't know. I haven't spoken to him since the funeral."

The water begins to warm. "It appears he's selling the house."

She raises an eyebrow, as if this is news to her. "I guess it is pretty big for him. Mariel always envied my having two daughters. She lost several children when they were babies. I don't know why they never adopted like we did."

I give her a look of surprise. "Your daughters look so much like you. I would have never guessed."

"That's what everyone tells me." She smiles like a true proud mother. "They do resemble me to a certain extent."

Adoption. Hmm. "I don't mean to pry, but...?"

I clamp down on my nosey question. It's not fair to put her on the spot and curiosity does indeed sometimes kill the cat. Or bring a dark wizard into your world.

"I don't have many secrets at my age, Summer," she says with a soft chuckle. "There's a bit of mental illness in my family, and although at times I've felt a little crazy myself, it seems to have skipped me. I simply couldn't imagine taking the chance and passing it on to a child."

Boy, I can understand that. "How long has your husband been gone?"

"Oh, it's been many years now. I know how Kaan feels—this house is too big for me—but I can't leave the memories, you know? It's probably difficult for him to live there without Mariel, but worse to think about leaving. The house belonged to her family, and since there's none of them left, I guess he figures it's best to sell it and move on."

"I didn't realize it was a family estate."

"The house is over a hundred years old, and previously, Mariel's ancestors built a different home on it, I believe. I think she said it burnt down in a fire, and some of her great-grandparents rebuilt it into what it is now."

"So, you think Kaan will go somewhere else?"

She waves a hand in the air, glancing out the window. "I have no idea. Why all this interest in the house? Are you in the market for one?"

When I glance at her, she winks. "Just curious. You know I love old houses and the history behind them."

She sits on the toilet seat lid and leans forward. "You know, a great-grandparent of Kaan's was an early explorer who came across the United States to this area. I believe he was one of the first to stake out Raven Falls. In fact, if I remember correctly, I believe he lived in a cabin on your land. Lost his wife, so it was just him and two sons."

My interest is peaked—and not in a good way. One of Kaan's ancestors might have lived in my cabin? Yikes.

The water begins to boil. I remove my hands, shutting off my fire element. I don't want the water to scorch my dear client. "Was his wife in the group that disappeared without any reason?"

I don't mention the evil in the woods—the Master— because that would no doubt scare her, and who knows if she even believes in such stuff, even as open-minded as she is about witchcraft and magick?

"It's quite an interesting story, from what I understand," Mrs. Sorensen says. "He and his wife traveled up from Mexico. Took them years before they ended up in this area. They had two sons, and he took the boys north of here on a trip. He was a botanist or something and was creating a book on the trees and fauna. When they returned, everyone was gone, including his wife."

I do a mental head slap. *The journal.* "How awful for him and his children."

"I believe him and the two boys were the only survivors. It's sad."

I dry my hands and help her stand. "Would you like us

to stay until you're done? Just to make sure everything's okay?"

She goes to a small transistor radio on the vanity—I bet Hopper would love to get his hands on that—and turns to a classic station. "That'd be lovely dear, but I know you have other things to do. How about I text as soon as I'm out to reassure you I'm okay?"

"If I don't hear from you in half an hour or so, I'll be back to check on you."

She hugs me and I let myself out of the bathroom.

Hopper is nowhere to be found downstairs, so I figure he's waiting in the van. I close the front door behind me as I step onto the porch.

Hopper's at the bottom of the steps. My heart nearly stops when I see who's joined us.

Near the fountain is Fontaine.

15

"I believe you have something that belongs to me," he says. "I'd like it back."

I fly down the steps. "Leave us alone."

Hopper touches my wrist with his fingertips. "What is it you think I have?"

"You were at my estate sale, weren't you? There was a book—a family heirloom—and several boxes of jewelry. It was a mix up—none of that was supposed to be sold."

He takes a step toward us and I put my arm out, as if that'll protect Hopper, "Stay back."

"If we return the items," Hopper says, "will you leave us alone?"

One corner of the wizard's mouth twitches. "I have no beef with either of you. I simply want my wife's belongings."

I know which book he's talking about—the journal. "I know what you are, so forgive me, if I don't believe that's all you want."

Another twitch. "And I know what *you* are, little Firestarter. You and your sisters cannot begin to fully understand or contain the beast in the woods."

"The beast?" Hopper asks.

"I'll explain later," I say, but what I'm thinking is, *blood and bones, why did Fontaine have to bring* that *up*? "I suppose you'd like to be the one to raise it. You should know it's just as likely to destroy you as it is us."

A hint of sadness enters his eyes. "My soul is already dammed, but I have no desire to rush head long into the fires of hell. Contrary to what you believe, all I want is to be left alone, but I require my items first."

"Why, because you know I'll figure out the truth of Mariel's death?"

He cocks his head, surprise in his obsidian eyes. "What do you know about that?"

"I know it wasn't due to natural causes and you've been working dark magick for a lot of years. I know about your ancestors that escaped the Master—the beast—three hundred years ago, and I'm wondering what kind of sacrifices you've been making to it."

I'm totally guessing about all of that, hoping to trigger an admission about who he is and what he's done to Mariel.

He steps forward, and my palms heat, ready to throw fire. "I want the journal back. The jewelry, too. Deliver it tonight and you'll never see me again."

Before we can respond he disappears into thin air.

"Where did he go?" Hopper looks around frantically.

"He's an expert at his craft, I'll give him that. Come on." I drag Hopper to the van. "We need to get out of here."

Back at Conjure, Autumn is minding the shop, Spring is baking. We take over kitten duty, and I hunt down Winter. She and Dad are sitting on the porch. "Did you finish reading the journal Hopper brought?"

The afternoon is growing hot and I wonder how she can

stand wearing black clothes all summer. Godfrey sits on one of the steps, licking his paws. "Not yet," she says. "Why?"

Hopper and I bring her and Dad up to speed on what happened. Spring ventures out and leans on the railing as I'm telling our story. "He wants the journal, along with the jewelry, and if it will get him off our backs, I'll give it to him."

"You really think he'll leave,"—Spring's eyes shift to Hopper then return to me— "us alone if he gets his stuff back?"

She emphasizes *us*, but what she means is Hopper.

I don't think he will, but I ask, "It's worth a try, isn't it?"

Dad leans forward in his chair. "Gather the man's possessions and I'll take them to him."

A part of me feels relieved he'd do this for me. Another feels fear. I can't send him to deal with Fontaine.

We lost Mom less than a year ago, and if anything were to happen to him, I couldn't stand it. "I'm not taking it directly to him, and neither are you. I have a plan."

Hopper cradles Chopin, the little orange tabby who is a big eater but still too skinny. "I'm not letting you go alone if that's what you're thinking."

My knight in shining armor. I know he's dying to ask more about the "beast" in the woods, but he's holding back on it. My heart swells a little.

Dad always says a plan is only good if it can be changed. "None of us are going to be there when Fontaine shows up. I'll take the items to a neutral location and he can meet me there. Or I'll leave them, then let him know where and he can pick them up."

Godfrey speaks inside my head. *Bad idea, human. You're not smart enough to take him on.*

"Do you really think he won't come after us, regardless?"

Winter asks again. "You know better than that, Summer. Black magick wizards don't just turn the other cheek."

Spring sits on the wooden porch boards and pets the kittens in the box. "I agree."

I get a text from Mrs. Sorensen—she's okay. At least one thing's going right today. "I may have let myself into his house and nosily slipped around, but he's the one who showed up at Hopper's store ready to do him harm. If anyone should be pissed it's me. The only thing Fontaine is worried about is me figuring out what happened to his wife."

Hopper starts feeding Chopin, "What is the beast he was talking about? You said he was sacrificing things to it?"

My sisters look at me with fear in their eyes.

Yes, the cat's out of the bag.

Okay, so we're having *that* discussion now. "The reason so many have disappeared from this area over the centuries is due to something we believe is sort of like a demon," I tell him. "We've managed to contain it in the earth under the forest. I have a theory Mariel's death involves Kaan, his ancestors, and or something with this beast. That's why Kaan's desperate to get that journal back. It might hold answers. Mariel could be some form of immortal who is tied to what happened here in the 1600s, or he's been using his powers to keep her young and beautiful. I don't know." I shuffle my feet. "She wasn't aging, he's into black magick, none of their three children lived past infancy. Hate to say it, but maybe they were sacrifices. It all has to be tied together; I just don't know how."

I sense everyone's *eww* response. *Right there with you.*

"Immortal?" Dad looks pensive rather than shocked. He's a shaman, after all and has seen and heard some pretty weird things. "I thought this Mariel died?"

"Maybe her magick ran out," I say. "Or Kaan's did. Perhaps they didn't have the right sacrifice this time. Anyone else have a theory?"

Dad sits back and looks toward Spring's gardens. "Black magick does involve necromancy. What if, each time Mariel dies, Kaan raises her? You could be right about the sacrifices. He needs a life to exchange for hers."

We all look at him and I feel our dismay ratcheting up a notch.

"Some believe the dead know all," Winter says softly.

"What if they were trying to find out what happened to the lost colony?" I add. "Or, they've been trying to bring someone from it back?"

As if I've opened a portal into another world, I feel the one I'm in begin to slip. Everything grows fuzzy, the world spins. I grip the arms of my chair, hearing Hopper yell my name.

In the next instance, I'm falling.

16

"*Y*ou have to do it."

I'm Mariel again. My hand is hers as she grips Kaan's arm.

"There's no guarantee, my love." His voice is marked with pain and fear. "Surely there's a better way!"

My vision is faulty, I can't seem to keep my eyes open. Anemic light from a frail moon falls over us and I have the sensation I'm lying down, but whatever I'm on is hard and cold like the ground.

"The beast is *coming*," my voice hitches. "It's growing closer. I'm the only one who got away. You can't let him have me!"

Shadows move, then a flash of steel, a knife rising in the air as if held by an invisible hand.

"Promise me," I say, barely more than a whisper. "You must promise."

"I love you." Kaan's voice is far away, as if in a vacuum. "I won't let him have you."

"Swear you'll bring me back!"

The knife flashes, trembling in the air over me, and I feel something cold grab my leg.

I scream.

Claws tear at both legs now, searing heat flooding through me with a frozen edge. I'm paralyzed, the struggle only inside my mind.

They reach into my belly, squeezing my organs. "Now!" I yell. "Do it now!"

"I love you!" I hear Kaan shout, nothing more than a very distant murmur. "I promise!"

It's nearly at my heart now, ready to consume it.

Time freezes, much like my body. Another flash of the knife, this time as it plunges through the air and into my chest.

I'm falling. The beast reaches for me, but he can't quite catch me. Can't reach my heart as the physical thing stops beating, and I feel Kaan's love wrapping around me, a protective barrier as I leave this world...

I snap out of the vision as my physical body in present time pitches forward. I'm tumbling to the porch when strong hands grab me.

A shaft of sunlight grazes my face and the world stops spinning. I'm back in my chair, my eyes focusing on tiny specks of dust floating in a beam of light. My heart jumps rope in my chest before resuming its normal rhythm.

Hopper's in front of me, his hands on my arms pressing me into the seat. On either side of him are my sisters. Behind them stands Dad.

"Another vision?" Hopper's face is tight with tension.

Nodding, I feel my stomach turn over on itself. As if with super human strength, I push his hands away, stand, then run into Conjure's bathroom.

I barely make it before I heave up the contents of my

stomach. When I'm done, I wipe my face and find Winter in the doorway. Spring rushes past her with ice water and I sink to the floor, my back against the wall.

Taking a sip, nearly too weak to hold the glass, but Spring keeps her hands on it, helping me. The cold water cools my burning throat. For a moment, I fear I'm going to vomit again, but I don't. It settles and so does my chaotic energy.

I touch the Phoenix at my throat, and the citrines of the eyes buzz under my fingertips. I feel their energy working on my digestion, calming the rough seas of my stomach.

"Did you see the future?" Winter asks.

"The past. Mariel and Kaan again."

"But how?" Spring asks. "You weren't touching them or anything of theirs."

"I must have a connection to her now. This one was bad. Really bad."

Spring sits next to me, taking the glass from my shaking hand. Winter leans against the sink. "Tell us," she says.

Hopper appears in the doorway. "Are you okay?"

How many times has he asked me that the past two days? I feel sorry for him, feeling how palpable his worry is as he stands there not knowing what to do for me. Realizing there's nothing he *can* do.

"I will be." I take another sip, hand the glass to Spring and rest my head on the wall, closing my eyes. "Mariel's tied to the Master. In this vision, it came for her. And, it nearly got her. If it wasn't for Kaan..."

I sense Winter crouch near me. "What was he doing?"

Like a dream, the bits and pieces seem to be scattering. "He was...killing her, but it was saving her."

Heavy silence descends and I flip my eyes open, afraid

I've fallen into another vision. Everyone is still there, all of them looking at me as if waiting for an explanation.

"I know that doesn't make sense, but she wanted Kaan to do it in order to keep her from the demon. She said, 'I'm the only one who got away' and she kept calling it the beast."

"That's how it was referred to in the journal," Winter says. "The beast who rose from the earth and stole the people."

"Kaan called it that, too," Hopper adds.

"But the author of the journal and his sons weren't taken." I repeat some of my conversation with Mrs. Sorensen. "According to her, they were on a trip north when it happened."

"Mariel's tied to the master," Spring says. "But how would killing her keep her *from* him?"

I rub the spot in the center of my chest, feeling the black magick clinging to me like a sticky substance. "Everything is backwards," I murmur. "She survived when she should've died. Killing her saves her. The master wants her because she escaped him the first time." I shake my head, not sure I'm making sense.

Winter lays her hand over mine. "Summer, I haven't finished reading yet, but two days after they returned, one of the kids found a baby in a cabin. A girl."

Parts of the story snap into place. "She survived when she should've died," I repeat. "That was Mariel?" I meet Winter's eyes. "The boy that found her, what was his name?"

"The author of the journal only referred to his son with initials, A. E. Maybe that *was* the kid's name." she shrugs. "I mean the dad only used A as his first name."

"What about the other boy?" Spring asks.

"Same. He referred to him as A. Jr."

"And the baby?" Hopper asks.

Winter screws up her face. The blood is rushing in my ears. "The author referred to her as Mary Ellen."

My head is so full, it takes a second for the two names to click.

As if helping me, Winter supplies, "Mariel. Mary Ellen."

"By the goddess" I swear softly.

"The owner of the journal," Hopper says. "What was his last name again?"

"Finton," Winter spells it out.

"I need a piece of paper and a pencil."

He turns and Winter rushes after him. Spring helps me stand and we follow.

By the time the two of us reach the kitchen, Winter is slapping a piece of scrap paper on the table.

"What is it?" I ask Hopper.

He spells out Fontaine, then Finton underneath it. He begins crossing out letters—f, n, t—everything they both contain. When he's done, there are only two left.

He circles each and raises the paper to show me.

"A and E," I murmur.

He tosses the pencil down. "A.E Finton is Kaan Fontaine —the boy who found Mariel—Mary Ellen—still alive."

17

I know why Kaan resorted to black magick. He's spent the past three-hundred-plus years trying to keep Mariel out of the grip of the master.

"Hestia help me," I say, sitting at the kitchen table. I'm still weak and overwhelmed from what these two have done. Who Kaan and Mariel really are. "All these years, the Master has been coming after her again and again—the one who got away—and Kaan's been trying to keep her alive, so it can't have her."

"How is that possible?" Hopper asks.

Poor guy. He has to be even more confused than the rest of us.

"How is it she survived in the first place?" Winter adds.

There are certainly more questions than answers. "They're both cursed." I pick up the pencil and retrace the letters above the last names. "He loved her so much, he did whatever it'd take to keep her from the demon. He had to be the one to kill her to keep her soul attached to his."

I'm totally winging it, but it seems right. "I don't know for sure how many times they've done this, but I think something went wrong with this attempt. Either that, or Kaan still plans to raise her from the dead."

"So we're saying these two people have been alive, or died and come back multiple times in the past three hundred years?" Spring asks.

Our father paces next to me. "This is very dark magick. It's not something I want you to mess with."

"But this could help us save Mom," Spring says, a fierceness in her eyes. "If we can raise her and keep her from the demon—"

"No." Dad stops pacing, holds up both hands, and shakes his head. "What's dead should stay dead. We will not bring your mother back to the land of the living. You must find a different way to release his hold on her."

"We need to talk to Fontaine," I say.

Hopper seems to be taking all of this in stride. "Where are the books?" he asks. "I'll take them and the jewelry to Fontaine. Summer can come and ask questions."

Winter stands beside our father. "We know his secrets now; he won't be happy. I have to agree with Dad, I don't think we want to get involved with whatever it is they've been doing to raise her every time she dies. There's something very twisted about all of it, and we can't trust Kaan to tell the truth."

She's right, but how can I let this go? I know Spring feels the same way. "If there's any chance he can tell us more about the demon, it can only help our quest to save mom. I'll promise we'll leave him and Mariel alone. We won't interfere with whatever dark magick they're working, but he may know if there's a way to save mom."

"If there was," Dad says, "Don't you think he would've used it already to save the woman he loves?"

I never argue with my father—it's a losing proposition—

but today, I can't seem to stop. "The key lies in why the demon didn't get Mariel in the first place, I know it. If Kaan can tell us that, it may lead to the answers we need."

At this point, it's Spring and I against Winter and Dad. I glance at Hopper. "You should bow out on this; in fact, I prefer you do. We've already put you in danger—*I have*. I don't want you anywhere near this guy."

He reaches over and chucks me under the chin as if I'm a small child. "I appreciate the concern, but I'm too far in to let it go now. And there's no way on God's green earth I'm letting you walk into the lion's den without me."

Winter shakes her head and gives an audible sigh. Telepathically, she says to me, *you're a fool if you don't keep him.* "I'll get the books, but I'm not giving them to you until I've read the rest of the journal. I want to know how it ends."

"How much more do you have?" Hopper asks.

"Probably a hundred pages, so I should be done by tonight."

There's no point in arguing or demanding she bring it now. She turns on her heel and walks out the back door, letting the screen smack hard. I hear the kittens on the porch. "Blood and bones, we forgot about them."

Hopper and I rush to take care of them. Dad disappears. Spring heads to the front to let Autumn know about everything that's happened.

As I sit with the kittens and Hopper on the porch, I slowly move the rocking chair and let the sun warm my cold bones. I fear my plan may backfire, but what choice do I have? If I want answers, the dark wizard is the only one who can give them to me.

I pray to Hestia, my ancestors, and any other forces who might keep Hopper safe. I need all the help I can get.

18

I have two clients for energy sessions that afternoon. I consider canceling them, especially since I'm still weak and my brain is spinning in all kinds of crazy directions, but helping others is exactly what I need.

When you give a healing, you get one. That's one of the things my mother taught me. She had a gift for knowing what was wrong with people, and what could bring their bodies, emotions, and minds into alignment. That was the true path to prosperity, and she always told me—alignment with the universal Source of all life.

My first is a woman in her thirties whose husband cheated on her. They have two young children, and although she loves him more than anything, she's struggling to get over the heartbreak and trust him again.

The emotional pain is leading her to have panic attacks. When she arrives, she's breathing heavily, as though she's run here instead of driving. Immediately, I get her on my table and have her close her eyes as I send an imaginary thread of energy from the back of her heart to the earth. Getting out of my own head so I can help her resets my energy, and I, too, send an imaginary cord into Mother Earth.

Over the next hour, I place various crystals on her, focusing a lot on rose quartz and rhodonite around and on her chest. Selenite palm stones go in her hands and red jasper between her knees. I play soothing nature sounds and later on do a visualization to aid her heart.

There are points where she cries from overwhelming emotions, and I hand her tissues. I invoke a beautiful green light to fill her and strengthen her soul, clearing out her heart chakra and filling it with love and compassion, forgiveness and strength. Her breathing returns to normal and even deepens.

At the end, her tears have dried. We chat for several minutes and I get her some water. Her color is better, her energy levels strong again. She thanks me profusely and we set a date for the following month for her next session.

My second client is a man in his fifties who's lost his job, is overweight, and is fighting high blood pressure and diabetes. His wife insists he come to me to relax, if nothing else. He's a grumpy old bugger, but I know he enjoys these appointments even though he claims to not believe in them.

Once he's on my table, I see his heart chakra is out of balance, along with his solar plexus. I use bloodstone, emerald, and chalcedony on and around him. I use my hands to bring light into his system, activating the stones, cleaning his blood and helping the flow of his fluids. It also supports his digestive tract. He falls asleep, and his snores echo in the room. I smile to myself. Rest is the best medicine to bring the body into alignment.

I text Winter when I'm done to see how she's doing. She doesn't return it, meaning she's not finished reading the journal.

My head is clear now and I feel stronger, thanks to the healings. I hope I can keep this clarity dealing with Fontaine. I need to decide how to contact him and where to tell him I'll leave the stuff. The thing is, I need to talk to him, too. I have too many questions only he can answer.

I take time to post to our social media accounts, like comments, respond where necessary, and help Spring when she gets busy.

Autumn is babysitting the kittens. Hopper went back to his shop. Since we have Fontaine's ultimatum to return Mariel's items by the end of the day, I figure Hopper's probably safe for now. Fontaine won't risk hurting him if he thinks he'll get his possessions tonight.

After completing my work, I feed the kittens and ignore Godfrey as he follows me, berating me for my inability to think through what I'm doing with the dark wizard. After I ask what his solution would be, and why my mother was dabbling in dark magick, he falls silent and disappears. Big help he is, genius reincarnated...*not*. After all, he was her familiar. He must know what she was doing.

Closing time is just around the corner as I sit in the office to search online for a number to call Kaan. I may not be as smart as Godfrey but I'm not willing to go to Fontaine's property again. Like my original plan, I intend to draw him to a neutral location.

He wants Mariel's things; I want answers. I believe we can come to a compromise, but just in case, I want things stacked in my favor.

My search turns up blank. There's no listing for Kaan and Mariel Fontaine. Perhaps they only use cells, but I find nothing for those either, only the address for their house.

Outside of Mariel's obituary, there's no more information. This makes me suspicious. They must've really been introverts, and considering what I believe about them, that doesn't surprise me. How awful it must be to die and come back to life, knowing all your friends and family are gone. That any aquaintances you make now will pass before you do.

Mrs. Sorensen. She claimed to be friends with Mariel and she's still alive.

I call her, and she answers after a couple rings. "Summer! I was just thinking about you. My friend, Karen, is having health trouble. I wonder if you have time in your schedule to see her for a session soon."

"Of course, I'll check my calendar." I already know I'm booked the next six weeks, but maybe I'll have a cancellation and can squeeze Karen in. "Say, do you have the Fontaine's number?"

"They never had a landline. Mariel hated phones, said the ringing always startled her so bad she'd have heart palpitations. She was very eccentric like that."

"How about a cell?"

"No, they didn't have those either. Or computers. I guess, since they didn't have any family, they didn't really see the need for that stuff."

"What about for emergencies?"

"Odd, I know. Even I'm not that far out of touch, but that's how they were." She hesitates a second. "Summer, what's going on?"

I consider whether I should make up another lie about the house. Maybe it's better to just avoid any sort of explanations. Besides, I suck at lying. "How did you get messages to her?"

"We chatted practically every morning, walking the trail that runs behind our homes. I couldn't always go far because of the arthritis, but on a good day, we could walk for miles. It was wonderful exercise. Talked about pretty much everything under the sun. You would've thought we could fix all the world's problems with the ideas we had."

"What trail?"

"It's really nothing more than a footpath at the back of the properties. It starts half a mile or so northwest of my property and runs almost to your hot spring, passing the public park. I believe your sister runs on it with her dog—I see them occasionally. At one time it probably went all the way to your place, right through the national forest behind the Harrington Farm, but once they put in those new condos on the edge of town, it got cut off."

I make a note on the paper in front of me. Park. That might be a good place to meet. "Huh. I didn't know that."

"What is it you need to call Kaan for, my dear? You know, I can walk to his house and deliver a message if that would help."

"Hopper accidentally got some of Mariel's personal belongings at an estate auction over the weekend. I'll just drive by later and drop them off. No big deal. Thanks."

I abruptly say goodbye and disconnect. The last thing I need is for Mrs. Sorensen to get involved in all of this.

Sitting to think for a moment, I draw circles around the word *park*, then call the realtor. She should have a way to get a message to Fontaine.

Her phone goes directly to voicemail and I debate leaving a message since she may be off work already. Depending on when she checks her messages, it might not get to Kaan in time.

Autumn appears at my right shoulder. "You know, I could project to his house and tell him to meet you at the park, or wherever you decide."

Startled, I whip my head around to look at her. "Are you reading my mind?"

She laughs. "I heard you talking to Mrs. Sorensen, and you circled the word park."

Her idea isn't bad, to be honest. "This may sound paranoid, but what if he's able to trap your astral self there? His skills are impressive, and who knows what he has up his sleeve? Could be too dangerous."

"This whole thing is," my sister says.

She and I look at each other, contemplating the best way to avoid it. Needless to say, neither of us seems to have a remedy.

Winter squeezes into the small office, a stack of books in hand. "Finished. Some pretty interesting stuff in this journal, but Merlin's beard, it's a hard one to read. The way they spoke and wrote during that time period is plain weird."

Autumn tidies a collection of invoices in our product fulfillment basket. I'm falling behind on shipping product orders, and a new layer of guilt is added to my current one. Depending on how things go with Fontaine later, I better come back here and get caught up.

"Anything we should know before we return it?" Autumn asks.

"If I had time, I'd copy the journal so I could review it in more depth," Winter says. "The stuff about the colony is fascinating, but unfortunately there isn't as much about the people as there is the animals and plants. He did mention an old woman who lived alone in one of the cabins. Might've been mine, by the way he described it near the forest line. She was apparently deep in the woods the day everyone disappeared, and the beast didn't get her either.

"But she wasn't considered part of the colony. From the sounds of it, she might have been a witch. In fact, I'm pretty sure she was. Apparently, Mr. Finton and his sons gave Mary Ellen to her to raise. He mentioned how the witch went to the hot spring every full moon and stayed the whole night. She didn't seem to age, and she brought the child with her. He said the water was bewitched, but it improved the baby's health, who was sickly and small for her age."

"So Mary Ellen grew up with a witch?" I ask. "Light or dark?"

Winter shrugs. "No way to be sure, but he mentioned that she used herbs, flowers, and tree bark to treat sick people in the colony. He was very interested in the properties of all of those, so naturally, he wanted to know why and how they worked."

"No mention of what happened to her? Did she raise Mary Ellen to adulthood?"

"The only other thing is that when she started walking, she followed his son—the one who found her—everywhere. The entries stop about ten months after the colony vanished."

I sit back in the chair and wiggle the pen I'm holding. I lock on to it with my eyes, and make it hover over my open palm. Telekinesis is not one of my strong skills, but I work on it and find it helps hone my focus at times.

"I don't want any of us to have to go to Fontaine's house to return his stuff, but he doesn't have a phone—landline or cell—nor email. His realtor isn't available to contact him, and I don't want to involve Mrs. Sorensen, even though she knows him and offered to help. I'm flat out of ideas on how to communicate with the man other than pure magick. Any suggestions?"

Autumn glances at Winter. "I offered to astral travel to his house."

Winter leans on the filing cabinet, twirling a piece of

curly hair between her fingers. "I can make myself invisible and take a written message to slip under his front door."

Spring appears in the doorway. "We're all locked up. Dad and I are ready to go." She sets Mariel's necklace on the desk. "Dug this up for you."

"Thank you, sister. Do you think he'll have his place warded just in case?" I ask all of them

Winter flips the lock of hair over her shoulder. "I would."

"You can't meet him on neutral ground if you can't tell him where that is," Autumn says. "And if he really wants his stuff, he won't try anything until he's got it. We should be more concerned with protecting ourselves once we hand it over."

"Dad and I have that covered," Winter informs us.

I want to ask exactly what that entails, but before I do, Autumn's body slumps to the floor.

"Holy Hestia," I say reaching for her. Most people might freak out, thinking my sister fainted, but I know better. "Tell me she did not just astral project there!"

Winter laughs and Spring helps me prop Autumn against the desk.

We stay put, kneeling beside her until she returns to her body. She takes a deep gasping breath and her eyes fly open.

Relief spreads through me and a trace of black magick tingles the back of my neck. Autumn looks at me and smiles. "Message delivered. I told him to meet us at the park up the road from his house in thirty minutes."

"By all that's holy," I say. "Thank you, but please don't do that again."

"You're welcome." She reaches out and pats my cheek. "Have a little faith, sister."

Winter pushes off the filing cabinet. "Let's get going and pick up Hopper on the way."

19

*H*opper is ready when we arrive.

With him, the four of us, and Dad, sitting room is limited. Winter drives and Dad, in the passenger seat, hands the kittens to Hopper when he sits next to me.

Along with them, we have our familiars—Shade, the ghost cat, lies in Winter's lap. Spring's mockingbird, Hoax, hops between the seats. Sirius paces between the windows in the back while Autumn gripes at him about leaving muzzle prints on the glass. Cinders swings on the bar in his fireproof cage that hangs from a hook in the cargo area.

Godfrey, not to be left behind, lays on the dashboard, licking his paws and cleaning his face.

"So, what if Fontaine admits killing Mariel?" Winter asks. "I mean, is there really anything we can do about it?"

Spring leans forward in her seat, "Tristan is meeting us there. He'll stay hidden, but just in case Fontaine confesses anything illegal, he'll be ready to take him into custody."

I doubt Kaan will allow himself to be arrested, but I appreciate her trying to help. Tristan, too. "Mostly, I need to know the truth. If Fontaine has been using black magick to try to save Mariel, maybe he needs help, and even if he *is* guilty of raising her from the dead, there's not much we can do about that."

Hopper stays quiet, so does Dad. I wonder what's running through their minds.

The Tina Cloister Memorial Park, nestled between Mrs. Sorensen's house and the Fontaine mansion, spreads over an acre or so of ground with a tall hill in the center. It's well-appointed with trees, bushes, and blooming flowers, named for the woman who originally had a large atrium here. There's a koi pond, a large white gazebo, and a look-out spot on top.

Parking spaces are limited, as if those who designed the lot didn't want it to turn into a tourist destination. An absence of playground equipment keeps it from being a hot spot for toddlers. Most parents take their kids to the Raven Falls park downtown.

Luckily, there's one open and Winter pulls in. A young man walking a German Shepherd goes by on the sidewalk. A couple on a bench under a nearby willow tree stare dreamily at each other. A mother with a couple pre-teen children are near the pond, feeding the fish.

"We don't want collateral damage," I say. "We may need to use a little magick to get these people to move along."

Dad absentmindedly strokes Godfrey, who looks at him with annoyance. "I'll handle them. If I can't get them to leave, I'll shield them."

"Thank you, Dad."

He reaches back and takes my hand. His is rough and wrinkled, several turquoise rings on his fingers. I don't worry about touching him—like my sisters, I don't get visions about him. I squeeze his fingers, the cool metal of his turquoise jewelry reassuring against my warm skin. "I love you, daughter," he says. "Be safe."

"Are we ready?" Winter asks. "Before I make you invisible, we need to figure out where everybody's going to stand."

The dashboard clock tells me we have ten minutes before Kaan is due. Sirius jumps into Autumn's lap, whining. He's far too big to be a lap dog and she nearly disappears under all that wolfhound hair. In my mind, it sounds like he's saying, "Going? Now? *Outoutout*. Walk? Smell... What is ... scent?"

She scratches around his ears and he pants. "We should form the five points of a pentagram and lock our magick together, like we do in the woods. Spring and Hopper need to be in the center, so that leaves us without the fifth point."

Hopper glances at the sleeping kittens in his lap. "I'll meet Fontaine in the center and give him his stuff back. Spring can stay at one of the points."

"No way," I tell him. "I don't even want you in the pentagram. You should stay in the van."

He looks at me with serious consideration in his eyes. "You know that won't happen."

Rats. I sigh. "I had to try."

"Tristan has magick," Spring volunteers. "He can hold the fifth if you want."

The mother and her kids finish and begin walking to the entrance of the park. That makes me feel better. Now if the couple would leave.

"Getting Fontaine into the center might be tricky—he'll be expecting it." Winter taps her fingers on the wheel. "Even if the five of us are invisible, he'll be able to feel the magick."

"We won't raise it until he's with you," Autumn says. Light through the van window brightens her red hair to orange. "We'll stay invisible and contain our magick until he's in the center of the pentagram."

"That might work." I finger the phoenix pendant. "I put a beacon spell on the journal and jewelry, so he knows where to find us. They'll give a magickal pulse he should be able to pick up on. I don't want to put him on the defensive if there's any chance I can get information about Mariel's tie to the demon. Hopper and I have the leverage with her stuff, so I'm hoping Kaan will divulge it. If he refuses, or tries any funny business, I'll say Cinders' name. That'll be the signal to raise the pentagram."

Nods and murmurs of agreements fill the van. Winter turns to look at us. "Grab hands."

We form a circle, Spring on one side of me, Hopper on the other. I'm wearing my fingerless gloves, so the Touch doesn't kick in.

I still feel a buzz of electricity from Hopper's skin through the lace and my heart beats faster. For a sweet moment, I want to burst out, "I love you," but bite my tongue. I do send him the mental message, along with a shy smile.

I can tell he's reluctant to grab me hard, afraid the lace won't be enough to protect me, so he rubs his thumb across my knuckles, that sweet familiar sensation sending more bolts of electricity zig-zagging up my arm and into my heart.

Godfrey reluctantly climbs into Dad's lap and yawns. I mentally lock onto Cinders' magick. Power flows from each of the animals into us sisters, our familiars giving an extra boost. I mentally tell Godfrey to give Dad the same.

He yawns again, looking at me through half-slitted eyes.

We can't hold this for long, but I revel in the fiery sensation of mine, feeling my power ratchet up several notches. I'm not sure what Hopper feels, but I imagine even he can sense an increase in energy. My magick turns protective, flooding his aura.

Dad says a prayer to our ancestors, spirit guides, and our higher selves, asking for blessings and guidance as we confront Kaan. He asks for what is hidden to be revealed, and to assist us to make sure justice is done for Mariel.

He also asks our spirit guides to grant us knowledge about the demon—Mariel's beast—that might allow us to help our mother.

When we're done, my body buzzes from head to toe as if I've stuck my finger in a light socket. Winter and Spring break their hold on Hopper and I and they hook hands. Winter says a spell over the others to create the invisibility cloak around them.

To the novice, it's an impressive sight. Hopper sucks in a quiet gasp before shooting me a hesitant grin.

I look at the map of the park on my phone and dole out instructions about where everyone should stand.

The center is actually at the top of the hill, and according to reviews, you can see the Pacific from the highest point on a clear day. I consider using it, but the rest of the group won't have a view of Hopper and I if I do.

I choose the gazebo instead for our meeting place. From there, it's easy to position the others so they form a pentagram. Tristan shows a minute later, receiving his own dose of invisibility along with instructions on where to go and what to do.

We fan out, each of our familiars following close by. Dad takes the kittens and sets them under a shady tree close to Autumn's spot. Sirius stands guard. Hopper brings the jewelry and books, and I carry Cinders in his cage.

I glance at my phone. Two minutes. Anxiety crawls up my spine and I try to shake it off. I'm hoping Fontaine will cooperate—that underneath the black magick he's actually a good person.

But what if he's not?

I can almost feel the seconds ticking by. I free Cinders and he hops to the top of it, spreading his wings and flapping as if he's shaking off his worries, too.

My sisters check in telepathically, letting me know they're ready. Hopper places the items on the ground and looks around. "Do you think he'll walk in like a normal person, or do that projection thing?"

"I suspect he'll be in astral form, but he can't carry his stuff out if he does that, so at some point, he'll have to materialize in physical form."

Hopper nods and continues to scan the area. He keeps his hands loose by his sides. He removes a pair of sunglasses from his shirt pocket and puts them on, and suddenly, I feel like I have a bodyguard as the mirrored lenses reflect my face back to me. "No matter what happens," he says, "I'll protect you."

My heart swells, and again, I feel the words *I love you* wanting to burst from my lips.

Timing, I remind myself. Those words are sacred. When you say them for the first time, it should be in a special place, intimate and memorable. This evening might be memorable, and the location special, but the situation makes it...

Well, I'm not sure what, but it's not conducive to spilling my heart to him.

"Thank you," I tell him, which honestly, sounds a little lame.

I can't help it; I check the time once more. We're at fifteen seconds. I reinforce my shields, extending them to Hopper.

He may believe he's protecting me, but I definitely am him.

In my head, I hear Winter's voice counting down. *Ten, nine, eight...*

I wonder if she's as anxious as I am. She never shows much emotion, good or bad, so it's hard to know, but I suspect putting us on alert to Fontaine's impending arrival is her way of controlling her worry and doubt.

Six, Five, Four...

I take a breath and hold it. Hopper touches my arm, a show of support.

Three, two, one.

Go time.

20

---

*T*he meeting time comes and goes.

The couple on the bench leave. Hopper and I look around, watching to see if Fontaine is walking into the park, rather than projecting here.

No Fontaine, either in flesh or spirit.

A light breeze ruffles my hair and I turn in a circle, smelling roses and jasmine. I lean over the gazebo's railing and look towards the hill, in case he's out there spying on us.

No dice. Unless his astral self is hiding in one of the trees, I can't pick up anything.

Minutes pass, and I hear my sisters in my mind discussing what's going on, or more specifically, what's *not*.

Are you sure you gave him the message? Winter asks Autumn.

I said it right to his face. Autumn sounds so calm.

Maybe he suspects our trap, Spring adds.

I think she's correct. *Let's give it a few more minutes*, I tell them.

Everyone falls silent.

Hopper gives me a couple questioning looks. I shrug. "Maybe he's not going to show."

"Something's not right." He continues to scan the park. "He's not coming, but that doesn't make sense. He wants his possessions back, doesn't he?"

"He probably assumes we're going to jump him. I'm not sure what we could do to a dark wizard, but I have the feeling he's been around a long time. He's not taking chances."

Five minutes pass, then ten. I sit on the gazebo stairs. Hopper next to me.

Patience is not one of my virtues. It takes all my willpower to wait another few minutes.

Finally, I admit defeat. "He's not coming. We might as well wrap this up."

Hopper rises, extending a hand to me. "Do you want to leave the stuff, just let him have it, and we go our separate ways?"

"I can't." Warily, I accept his hand and stand. "If he has information on the demon, we have to know."

Hopper picks up the books and jewelry. I put Cinders back in his cage.

Frustrated, I reach out with my magick in case Fontaine is listening or hiding somewhere waiting for us to leave. *I came here in good faith to return your items but I'm leaving now. I'm taking Mariel's things with me, so if you want them, you're screwed.*

I pick up the cage and am about to walk down the steps when icy prickles ripple over my skin.

Dark magick rushes at me, nearly knocking me off my feet. It clamps around my ribs, closing off my windpipe. Kaan's face floats in front of mine.

His mouth is distorted in what looks like a scream. His

eyes are wild, rolling up in their sockets. He seems to be reaching for me, and I back away instinctively, slapping at his hand.

Mine goes right through it, his astral self nothing more than air.

"Stop it! Are you trying to scare me?" I yell. "Well, it's not working. I know what you did for Mariel, how you tried to keep her from the demon—beast—and I only want a few answers. He has my mother, too. I need your help, but if you come after me or my sisters, it'll be the last thing you do."

His lips move, but there's no sound. Behind him, I see what looks like Mariel's bedroom.

A ghostly hand seems to be pulling at him, keeping him from communicating. He reaches out again, urgency in his face, and I realize what he's trying to say as I focus on his mouth.

Help.

A shudder races through me.

I grope for his hand, but once again my fingers pass through thin air. There's nothing to hold onto, to grasp.

And then, behind him, I see someone else.

A face stretched with anger... and evil.

I gasp and stumble back, finding myself against Hopper. He wraps his arms around me. "What is it?"

He can't see the wizard, can't see the ghost behind him.

"It's Kaan."

I search the man's astral face, feeling helpless. "What's happening? I don't understand."

His mouth moves again. *Help me.*

Before I can take another breath, the ghost snatches him away.

For half a second, I'm frozen, trying to make sense of it. I turn on my heels, breaking from Hopper's grip. "We have to go. Now."

Grabbing the cage once again, I send out a mental message to my sisters to meet at the van. "Hurry," I add.

When we're assembled there, I tell them what happened.

They gawk at me.

"You can't be serious," Winter says.

I'm still shivering from the encounter. "It was her. It was *Mariel*. She came for Kaan, and she's not happy. We have to get to his house. I think he's in real trouble."

My father shakes his head solemnly. "Smells like a trap to me."

"Me, too," Spring adds.

"It might be, but we can't take that chance. Something is wrong." Hopper may not be psychic, but he's nailed this one. "We have to help him."

Tristan has an arm around Spring. He looks at my Dad. "Let me go by the house, see if anything seems out of place. I'll call Spring if I think it's safe, you can decide what to do then."

I put Cinders in the van. "There's no time for that. We have to go now, all of us."

"I don't like it," Winter says.

Frustration boils inside me. I ball up my fists and put them on my hips. "I don't either, but we still have to do it, so get your butt in and drive."

She raises one elegantly arched eyebrow at me. Hopper takes my elbow to help me in and the others reluctantly climb in as well, familiars and all. A few seconds later, we're speeding to the Fontaine mansion. Tristan follows in his car.

"So, what's the plan?" Spring asks.

"Save Kaan from the ghost," I reply.

Autumn frowns at me. "I thought you said it was Mariel."

"It is. She's so angry. Something's not right though."

Dad holds Godfrey, who wriggles out of his hands and resumes his normal spot on the dash. As Winter swerves around a car, Godfrey digs his nails in.

Winter says, "Maybe her husband did kill her—not to save her but because of something else."

We're bewildered about Kaan being evil or not. "That's a possibility," I admit, but I don't want to accept it. I want to believe he and Mariel have such a deep love, that he'd never harm her. That he would do everything he could to keep her from the master.

Even delving into black magick.

But maybe I'm nothing more than a sappy romantic.

Hopper once more has the kittens in his lap. He catches my restless fingers. "Are you sure? Do you really want to help this guy?"

His face is grim, and his eyes tell me he's confused regarding my sudden about face with Fontaine. Just a few minutes ago, I was ready to trap the dark wizard in the pentagram and make him answer questions, afraid of his intentions. Now I'm rushing to his aid. "Yeah, I am."

He gives me a nod filled with grim determination. "I just want you to be safe."

I hook my fingers around his, feeling that tingling again right through my gloves. "Same goes for you. I don't know what we're facing, but it would help me to know you were in the van."

I see him set his jaw, resisting the idea once more. "Not my style to let my woman run into the jaws of danger while I sit back and do nothing."

My woman. A silly grin slips over my face, even as we

swerve again, and I have to grab his arm to keep from falling into the kittens. "You're very brave."

In my head, I hear my sisters chattering, clucking their tongues, saying *aww*, and in general, making me feel like I'm baring my soul to the world.

Hopper smiles. "Seems like that's you in this scenario."

I can tell he doesn't like it—the idea of me venturing into whatever's happening with Kaan and Mariel, but it isn't going to stop me.

We drive to the estate, Tristan following, and find the gate closed. We file out, and Autumn sends her spirit to the other side. Spring and Dad catch her physical body, and a few seconds later she's inside the small guardhouse. It takes her a minute to find the button, but finally, they swing open.

At the back of the van, I open the doors and release Cinders. He flies from the cage with a squawk. Sirius bounds out and follows me, my familiar flying ahead of us.

Autumn's astral-self steps from the guardhouse. "Let me go first," she says. "I'll scope things out. Be right back."

I don't want to wait, but it makes sense to let her get the lay of the land before we rush in.

Winter calls, "Everybody back in the van and I'll drive us up there."

We get in, Tristan and Hopper carrying Autumn.

Clouds move in from the ocean as the sun begins to sink. I stare at the mansion, trying to see through the front windows, but the curtains and shadows reveal nothing.

By the time we're at the porch, I'm buzzing with nerves. Autumn hasn't returned and fear starts to worm its way into my belly.

"Everyone sit still until Autumn returns," Dad warns.

"But," I start.

He gives me a hard look, shutting down the rest of my protest. "Stay put."

The next few seconds are excruciating. Is Kaan alive? Could Mariel's ghost kill him?

It's not out of the realm of possibility, although from what I understand about spirits from Winter she would have to be extremely powerful.

There's a sudden loud gasp as Autumn reenters her body and draws a deep breath in. Spring helps her sit up and she blinks several times, adjusting into the 3D world once more.

"What did you see?" I demand. "Is he in there? Is Mariel?"

She nods. "They're in a room upstairs. When I tried to get in, magick kept me out."

Hopper and I exchange a glance. "Mariel's bedroom," I say.

"I could hear Kaan trying to communicate with her, but her responses were... wailing," Autumn continues.

"Wailing?" Winter repeats.

"Almost like keening." Autumn rubs at her ears as if she can still hear it. "Reminds me of a banshee."

A new round of goosebumps covers my skin. Banshees warn of death. Is Mariel now one?

"Maybe she's not trying to hurt him." I feel more confused than ever. "Is she here to warn him that he's going to die?" I ask, looking at my sisters.

No one has an answer.

The sky suddenly fills with black birds—ravens. They descend on the lawn, fountain, gazebo.

I pointedly glance at Spring. Ravens often come to inform her about things.

"Why are the birds here?" I ask. "Another death harbinger?"

Her green eyes are brighter than mine and wide in her face. "Death is coming. Maybe for Kaan or maybe...us."

Heavy silence falls among us, and I can see in my father's face he wants us to turn around and get out of this place as fast as possible.

He has great wisdom, and I know he's right. This may be too dangerous for all of us.

But I can't walk away, can I? Can I leave him to whatever is coming—whether Mariel intends to kill him or something else does?

"Is it possible the demon is coming for him?" I ask my family.

Winter shakes her head. "It's locked in its prison."

"But Mariel's not," I say.

"What are you thinking?" Spring asks.

I feel it in my belly where the worms are churning, spreading fear throughout my whole system. "Mariel escaped the demon when she was a baby, and not this time. Kaan's magick didn't work, and the demon's angry. What if he's using her to bring Kaan to him for revenge?"

"Did you have a vision?" Autumn asks.

"I don't need a vision to tell me this."

My father's face seems to age even more. He looks toward the mansion. After a moment, he nods. "We must stop it."

A certain calm comes into my body then. Fear diminishes and I feel the rise of the fire inside me.

"Do you want me to cloak everyone again?" Winter asks quietly.

"Everybody but me," I tell her. "Kaan needs to be able to see me." *If he's still live.*

"What do you plan to do?" Hopper asks.

"Same as before. Find out the truth, if we can." Cinders flies from around the corner. Sirius stands at attention as though he hears something following the bird. "Beyond that, I'm not sure."

A second later, I'm shocked to see who appears, walking around the corner.

"Mrs. Sorensen?" Fear comes roaring back. "Oh no, what is she doing here?"

She stops at the bottom step, puts her hands on her hips, and calls, "Are you just going to sit there all night, or come in and help me?"

She doesn't wait for our response, stomping up the stairs and going right in the front door.

21

We scramble out of the van.

"Mrs. Sorensen," I yell, rushing into the foyer. She's already halfway to the second floor. "You don't want to go up there. It's dangerous."

"I know." She keeps climbing, barely looking over her shoulder at me. "Come on, Summer. I need your magick."

"But... But..."

I start up, my sisters filing into the wide-open foyer, as Mrs. Sorensen continues. Her hair begins to change, growing longer, whiter. Her summer outfit morphs into long flowing robes. Her wrinkled skin becomes youthful.

Shocked, I glance at my family. Hopper and Tristan have also entered but I don't have time to order them back out.

Once more, I begin climbing, trying to catch up to Mrs. Sorensen.

Or whoever she is.

"I don't understand," I say as we hit the top of the landing together.

Her eyes are as dark as my favorite chocolates. Her smile

serene. "I know you don't, dear, but I'll explain once we take care of this little problem."

From the end of the hallway I hear screaming, the keening Autumn mentioned. "What is she?" I ask. "Mariel? She's Mary Ellen, from the lost colony, right? But *what* is she?"

Mrs. Sorensen seems pleased I've figured this out. "I was at her birth, but she was frail, and I charmed her. The spell was supposed to help her grow healthy and protect her from her mother's bad karma. Instead, it protected her from much, much more."

"You're the witch from the journal. The beast didn't take Mary Ellen because of your spell."

"I was trying to help, and accidentally cursed the poor girl. I saved her from the beast but sentenced her to other unfortunate events. I wish I had more time to explain, but if you're going to save Kaan—and Mary Ellen in turn—we need to put a stop to what she's about to do."

The others have joined us. My father asks, "What exactly *is* she about to do?"

Mrs. Sorensen meets his stare. "The beast can't truly take Mary Ellen's soul unless she spills the blood of an innocent."

"Kaan isn't innocent," I argue. "He's a dark wizard, using black magick. He's resurrected her several times, if I'm not mistaken."

"Kaan—Alexander—rescued Mary Ellen that day so long ago, and he's continued to try and save her, going to certain extremes. But it was done out of love, not desire for power. He's never killed anyone, except her, and only because she begged him to each time the beast came for her."

A crashing noise comes down the hall from the

bedroom. We hear Kaan's voice cry out, before it's suddenly cut off.

Blood and bone. How could I have been so stupid not to connect the dots sooner? "We have no choice but to trust you. Tell us how we can stop this."

She looks down the hall. "Three times the beast has come for her and Kaan ended her life before it could get her soul. But that was the end of the charm. It couldn't last forever. I only wanted her to be an oracle to the world about the beast, what happened to the lost colony and tribes prior to that. When I realized it had given her a form of immortality, I encouraged her to be that voice. Things didn't work out that way, and Alexander was able to raise her three times. He couldn't this time, though, because the charm finally ran out. The only thing we can do is contain her spirit until we can find a way to destroy the beast."

"You want us to trap Mary Ellen's ghost?" Winter asks. "Like in some sort of container?"

Mrs. Sorensen nods, her white hair falling over her shoulders. "Do you still have her jewelry, Summer? The garnet ring?"

"It's in the van," Hopper says.

"Go get it, dear."

As Hopper jogs downstairs and out the door, she looks at me. "Are you ready?"

Am I? Cinders flies through the open door and up the stairs to land on the railing beside me. The phoenix necklace heats on my collar bone. "I've never done anything like this."

She smiles patiently. "Just follow my lead."

Robes flying, she rushes down the hallway past the library. I follow on her heels, praying to Brigid, Hestia, and any other goddess listening for assistance. I have no idea what we're about to walk into. No idea how to trap a spirit in a ring.

And honestly, I'm a little peeved Mrs. Sorensen didn't tell me who she really is.

All that flees my mind as magick sparks from her fingertips and the doors to the room open.

It's a disaster. The items on the makeup table, the fireplace mantle, and the reading table are strewn across the floor. Drops of blood form a trail leading to Kaan, whose pinned against the window overlooking the garden.

He seems to be held up by his neck, dangling off the ground. His eyes bulge, his mouth moving, but no sound is coming out as he struggles to breathe.

"Holy magick mushrooms," Winter says. She quickly moves next to the space in front of him. "Mariel—Mary Ellen—listen to me. No matter what the beast is telling you, he's lying."

Winter can see Mariel. I stand there and pretend I do, too. "She's right. Kaan—Alexander—loves you. He always has. And you him. He'd do anything for you—he *did*. Killing him won't bring you peace, it'll only seal your connection to the beast. You have to resist."

Kaan coughs and chokes, his body rising higher in response.

But the keening stops, leaving an echoing silence. I lean close to Winter and murmur, "Is she saying something?"

A shake of Winter's head. "We can help you," she tells Mary Ellen. "You don't have to spend eternity with the beast, or do what he says."

Winter gives a little nod to encourage me to keep talking to her.

"You could spend the afterlife with your children." I tell her. "Your babies want you."

It appears I've hit a nerve. Without warning Kaan drops to the ground.

Mrs. Sorensen rushes over, leaning down to help him. "I'm so sorry, Mary Ellen," she says to our ghost. "I never meant for the spell to do this to you."

Cinders flies in and lands on a bedpost. He squawks at me and I feel a surge of magick.

It gives me inspiration. I wave at Spring and Autumn to help, telepathically telling them my plan, as Dad helps Mrs. Sorensen pull Kaan from the window. I watch Winter as she stares at the ghost, making sure Mary Ellen doesn't follow them.

She doesn't. As our other two sisters join us, Winter and I hold out our hands. The four of us become a circle and I continue talking to Mary Ellen. "I know your babies meant everything to you. I know you wanted them to live, to ease your pain, but it wasn't their time. They're waiting for you on the other side of the veil, not the beast, if you let us help you. They want their mother to come take care of them."

In my mind, I hear Winter. *Keep it up. It's working.*

"All I've ever wanted is to get married and have children," I confess to Mary Ellen. "You lost your mother before you even got to know her, same with your children. They're all there, opening their arms to you. You can move on and see them. You can be a family again."

Hopper rushes in with the ring and I try not to shift my eyes to him. I focus on Mary Ellen, sending my magick into the ghost and hoping I can encourage her to not give in. From the corner of my eye, I see Hopper hand the ring to Mrs. Sorensen. She moves toward the circle.

I glance at Winter and send her a message. *Can we get her to cross over? Or do we have to trap her in the ring?*

Winter seems as torn as I am. We can't guarantee that

allowing Mary Ellen to cross will save her soul. And if we trap her, perhaps, we can truly free her down the road once we figure out how to destroy the demon.

But can we take that chance? Once again, there are too many questions and no answers.

If only Spring could freeze the ghost, or I could see into the future.

"That's it!" I say out loud. Mentally, I send a nudge to Spring, *can you freeze a spirit?*

Her gaze flicks to me, uncertainty in her eyes. *I can try.*

Do it.

She breaks our circle, raising her hands to the space where the ghost is. I can't see the magick leaving her, but I feel it.

We all glance at Winter. For half a second her face is blank, then a crooked smile spreads across it, "By the goddess, that worked."

Mrs. Sorensen hands me the ring. "How do we trap Mary Ellen inside?" I ask, a sick feeling in my stomach. There's something about doing this that feels off.

"I have a spell for it," she says.

The off feeling grows. I hand the ring to Winter. "Hold this for me."

Mrs. Sorensen frowns. "What are you doing?"

Stripping my gloves, I let them fall to the floor, then rub my hands, stimulating my palms. The heat of my magick flows. "Put my hands on the ghost," I tell Winter.

"Are you sure?"

"Yes."

My sister guides them to Mary Ellen. As they come into contact with the essence of the spirit, I flinch. Shivers race over my skin, punctuated by icy prickles.

Wait. What is this?

It wasn't only Kaan's black magick causing this sensation before.

It was Mary Ellen's, too.

"You're the one who turned to black magick first, aren't you?" I ask her ghost, even though she's frozen and I couldn't hear an answer anyway.

I glance at Mrs. Sorensen, then past her to Kaan. Their eyes tell me I'm on the right track. "You tried to keep her from it, didn't you?" I ask Kaan, as understanding floods my mind.

He lays in a heap but gives me a sad nod. His lips move, straining to say something, but no sound comes out. What is binding his voice?

He struggles to raise a hand; it keeps falling. Something is draining his magick as well as keeping him mute.

Then he shoots a very purposeful glare at Mrs. Sorensen, before his attention returns to me.

Godfrey jumps up on the bed. *Don't be so naive, human.*

Before I can put two and two together, and speak the truth, my connection with the ghost triggers the Touch.

22

The scenes fly by so quickly, I barely register them. Like a movie on fast forward, I see Mrs. Sorensen in her original form with long white hair and blue eyes.

There's a baby, a book of shadows, a cauldron steaming over a fire. In the background, I hear a woman crying, pleading for her baby. Mrs. Sorensen softly chants a spell under the sound. The child wriggles back and forth, fretting.

She picks up the infant and croons to her, even as she lets blood drip from a cut on her finger into the cauldron.

Oh no, I think. *Not Mrs. Sorensen.* As she puts Mary Ellen over her shoulder, I see she's wearing the garnet ring. The baby's eyes lock with mine.

Help me.

I snap back to the present with a gasp. I've stayed standing for once and disconnect from Mary Ellen's noncorporeal form.

As I sway, Mrs. Sorensen grabs me. I whirl, yanking out of her grasp. "How could you?"

She looks confused for a brief moment. "How...?"

It dawns on her that I know what she's done. She shoves me away and runs.

"If you can, cross Mary Ellen over," I tell Winter. "Let that poor soul go."

"But the demon—"

"Just do it!"

Spring throws a freezing jinx at Mrs. Sorensen. It hits her and rebounds, freezing Dad instead.

Hopper reaches out to grab the witch, and she flings magick at him, knocking him on his butt. Tristan yells for her to stop. Another flick of her hand and he spins and knocks into the bedside table.

I race after her fleeing form, sensing Autumn on my heels. Cinders flies ahead, and as we reach the landing, I expect to see Mrs. Sorensen rushing out the front door below.

Instead, she turns left and heads deeper into the house.

Down the stairs we race. By the time we reach the foyer, she's disappeared.

I close my eyes and hold still. I flair my magick out, connecting with my familiar. "Fire and ash grant my request. Let me see through the eyes of my pet."

For several heartbeats I feel as if I'm soaring, lifted out of my body. This is the closest I'll get to astral travel. My eyes become Cinders', and I spot Mrs. Sorensen hurrying out the back door of the mansion.

"This way." I motion for Autumn to follow.

We fly down a long corridor, through a small atrium with skylights, and onto a sizable patio. Across the lawn, Mrs. Sorensen hobbles for the edge of the property, her arthritis slowing her.

The trail. She's hoping to escape to her house.

No telling what she'll do if she reaches it. She may disappear forever, leaving me with no answers to my questions.

Raising my hands, I call on the heat within and imagine a ring of flames around the property.

Magickal fire bursts forth, creating a container she cannot get through without burning herself. She stops, turning to pin me with her gaze. She scans back and forth between me and the fire several times, speaking magickal spells.

It doesn't take long for her to realize she can't escape.

She searches for a weapon, wrapping a ward of protection around herself. Her hand shoots out toward a garden statue sitting next to a pot of blooming ivy.

It's heavy, but her magick is strong, levitating it. With a deft flick of her hand, she pitches it at me. A projectile.

I can float a pencil off my hand, but that's my limit. Luckily, Autumn practices all the time. She throws out a hand, blocking it and sending it to the ground. It busts into dozens of pieces.

I smile; the old witch glares.

I call the circle of fire closer, impelling Mrs. Sorensen to move in my direction. My sister doesn't say anything, doesn't move. She knows I have this.

As Mrs. Sorensen is forced to walk to me, she curses. I don't respond, my shields strong, but without warning, Cinders comes out of nowhere and knocks her down.

The ancient witch lands on her backside with a loud grunt.

"Thank you," I say to my familiar. "You get extra treats tonight."

I feel soft fur against my leg. Godfrey is at my feet. *She fooled you good*, he says arching against my leg. *You have to stop trusting everyone.*

I rein in the desire to boot the cat. Not hard, just enough to knock him off his pompous backside. "If you don't have anything constructive to say, kitty cat, go away."

He stops rubbing my leg, flicks his tail, and does just that. He doesn't walk far, sitting down next to Autumn, as if letting me know he prefers her over me anyway. Sirius is there too, tongue hanging out and tail wagging against the grass.

I'm only a few feet away from the altar where Kaan performed his rituals. This all started with the "charm" Mrs. Sorensen used.

A curse is more like it.

I step closer to the old witch. "What's your real name?"

She's still lying in the grass, as if she's given up. I hear Godfrey say to me, *don't get too close, she's still dangerous.*

The cat is right, but I sense all of the gumption is gone out of her. After three hundred years, I imagine she's tired.

She lifts herself onto her elbows, then to a seated position. She hangs her head over her knees. "Prudence, my family called me Prue. My name before that you wouldn't recognize. It was from an old, extinct language."

"Just how old are you?"

She lifts her head and looks at me. "Does it matter?"

"It does to me."

I'm not lying, I want to know. I considered her a friend.

She stares off into the distance, not seeming to see anything but the past. "I was born on a remote island in the Pacific. My maternal family existed for a millennium before our island was sunk under the sea. Few escaped—my mother was one of them. Eventually, I was the only one left and I ended up on this continent. I blended in with the natives for a while, until the first tribe was wiped out. I was the only one to survive."

She stands and I reinforce the container of fire. I sense the presence of the others joining us. "How?"

She shrugs, defeated. "It's something in my blood. I passed it on to Mary Ellen."

"Are you immortal?"

She shakes her head. "I've died many times, but the blood brings me back."

"Why turn to dark magick then?"

She holds out her hands in supplication. "I lost family, too, you know. My husband and child. They were all I had and I lost them the winter before the beast came. It used to come at regular intervals."

"Where you dabbling in necromancy when you took Mary Ellen from her mother?"

"Her mother was filled with disease. There was no way the babe would survive, so I shared my blood with her. A different kind of black magick. I could feel the beast was restless, wanting to rise, and I could never bring back George and little Geoffrey, so I was determined to save her."

"And you became her mother once she was found alive by Alexander."

Tears seep from the corners of her eyes and she wipes them away, looking toward the altar. "I screwed up. I saved and cursed her at the same time. As she grew, she became more and more attached to him. Eventually they married and I left the picture for a while. I searched for a way to kill the beast, but never found it."

Kaan steps forward. "You told us the only way to save her soul from him was with dark magick. You convinced her of that and she made me delve into it with her. Only, it didn't work this time."

She nods in agreement. "Three times and the charm of my blood ran out, regardless of what else we tried. Not only that, something has changed with the beast. It wants to rise but can't. The Whitethorne sisters have prevented that, like the prophecy says."

"What prophecy?" Winter asks.

"An ancient one from my line. It tells of four sisters who can contain the end of the world. I wasn't sure it was you." She points at us. "There have been others. None as strong. I was waiting until I knew for sure your power could stop that awful evil before I told you my story and offered my help."

"Why did you have to kill her?" Kaan asks, his eyes pleading with Prudence. "Why didn't you let me do it? Now the beast has her."

"*You* killed her?" Hopper asks, expressing all of our shock.

"It was my fault to begin with," the old witch says, as if reasoning with a child. "She got away because of *me*. We could no longer hold off the beast, but I thought if I cheated him one more time, maybe she had a chance to hang onto her soul. I think it put her in a state of limbo and was still able to use her. It wanted her to kill you"—she points at Kaan—"so it could take your soul, too. I hoped to contain it in the ring until I could figure something else out."

I feel a deep well of sadness and pain from her. She believed she was doing the right thing.

"Did you cross Mary Ellen into the light?" I ask Winter under my breath.

Her cool energy tingles against my fiery one. "It wasn't easy, but yes. Her soul is at rest."

Prue's shoulders slump with relief. Kaan weeps softly. "I don't want to live without her. She's always been with me."

"Mary Ellen is at peace," I tell him. "You should be happy for her."

"Thank you," he says in Winter's direction, then he pins

me with his gaze. "She was my everything. Can you imagine spending three hundred years with someone and losing them?"

I can, but know it will never happen.

"Are you semi-immortal like Prudence?" Autumn asks him.

"Only while his soul was tied to Mary Ellen," Prue volunteers. "It's the price he had to pay for the dark magick in order to always be there for her when the beast came."

I'm more determined than ever to destroy this thing we've imprisoned under our land. "Well, for now, you're both going to help us," I tell them.

All eyes turn to me, surprised.

None of the Whitethornes trust dark magick or those who dabble in it, but it's time we brought Prudence and Kaan into the light.

"I, for one, want to hear more about the prophecy," I tell the old witch. "Then you and Alexander will do everything in your powers, using *good* magick, to help us defeat this thing."

Her mouth trembles and another tear escapes. "That's all I've ever wanted, to defeat him to save the souls of my husband and son, of those wiped out before us. I'll do what I can to assist the four of you. I swear it."

"I'm going to hold you to that."

I release the magickal fire but stay on guard in case she tries to bolt. She doesn't.

Instead, she walks to Kaan—Alexander—and holds out her hands. "I'm so sorry. I truly tried to help both of you through the years."

It's as if all the air goes out of him. He drops his gaze, shoulders slumping. "I never knew my mother—she died before I was two. For years, you were the closest thing I had to one. Everything we did, you and I, was for Mary Ellen."

He resists, but she hugs him anyway. My sisters and I look at each other, silent communication passing between us. As screwed up as this situation with Prudence and Alexander is, without family—whether by blood or by choice—what are we?

My father gives me a nod of approval. Spring goes to Tristan and they embrace, Hoax flapping around on the ground and flinging curses at all of us. Godfrey has taken off and is nowhere in sight. Sirius heads to the bushes and marks a nearby tree.

Cinders rests on the altar, preening his wings. Shade, who I haven't seen since we entered the mansion, prances by me to get to Winter. There, he arches his back and rubs his ghostly body against her leg. She leans down and gives him a pat, fingers going right through his head.

"Everyone back to Conjure," Dad says. He motions at the group. "I think it's time for tea."

Spring claps.

"Can I have a moment alone with Alexander?" Prudence asks.

Warily, we file off, stopping at the edge of the yard to watch. They exchange words for a moment, but not loud enough for us to hear.

"I hope we did the right thing for Mary Ellen," I say to Winter.

She squeezes my arm as she heads for the van. "We did."

23

*L*ater that evening, we gather around the table in the shop's kitchen. Dad and Hopper have to put the leaf in. Tristan scavenges chairs from the cabins so we all have a place to sit.

Spring makes herbal tea and we eat the day's leftover bakery goods as we listen to Prue and Alex tell us their story.

Darkness falls deep and heavy outside. Cinders and Hoax are on the porch railing, squawks and squeaks letting me know they're having their own conversation. The kittens sleep in the corner, but St. Hildegard is in my lap. She's restless and I stroke her soft fur. Hopper sits close beside us, arm around the back of my chair, occasionally petting her as well.

With over three hundred years of history between them, it's a long and fascinating story. At the end, I understand why Prudence and Alexander resorted to using dark magick to save someone they both loved.

We must all face our personal demons. Even when we've acted out of the desire to save others, we sometimes create bad karma. After hearing the convoluted ups and downs of their time together, I'm more determined than ever not to mess with fate.

"What about the book of the dead the tribe had?" Winter asks Prue. "Did you ever see it?"

Her face is weary. She sips at her tea. "It was in my collection. I was trying to decipher it to see if I could stop the beast. I failed and walked away from all of my books and Grimoires. Away from my life in general, for a time."

Winter picks at the crumbs from her cookie. "I sure would like to get a look at it. Apparently, it's in a museum in Eugene."

"What good would that do?" Autumn asks. "Even if you could see it, you can't read it."

"I might be able to," Prue says. "I'm a bit rusty after all this time, but I could work on deciphering it again."

"How?" Hopper sits back in his chair. "It's not like they let you check things out and bring them home."

Winter gives him a sly smile. "I have ways of *borrowing* items, and of course, I would return it after we're done. Maybe we could copy it before we give it back."

"An artifact that old will require great care," Hopper says. He glances around the table. "You know I'm trained in handling rare antiquities such as books. I can help if you *borrow* it."

Dad nods, flipping one of his braids over his shoulder. "It's probably archived. I have a special relationship with the museum when it comes to native artifacts. Let me look into it and find out where they're keeping it. We can go from there."

We have questions for Prue and Alex and spend the next half hour asking them. Finally, we run out and she has one for us. "Will I still be able to use the hot springs, Summer?"

It's one of the keys to her longevity. Her unique blood

keeps her alive, but the miracle of that water keeps her healthy. "You must've been using it regularly before Mom's ancestors purchased the land," I say. "And since? I imagine you've been using it all this time. I doubt I can keep you from it."

"Once a month at the full moon," she admits. "Your mother knew I was sneaking out there but never said anything, bless her. Same for your grandmothers and aunties before you. But I don't want to trespass anymore, so I'd like to have your permission."

"In exchange for helping us stop the demon?"

"I give you my word."

"I want to help, too," Alex says. When we all look at him, he shrugs, "Without Mary Ellen, I have nothing holding me here, but neither do I have anywhere to go. I'm tired, and no longer immortal. I've already seen the world, done all a man might want to. I want to stay here for the rest of my life, in the family home, and do what I can to stop this thing."

We adjourn a few minutes later, everyone going their separate ways.

Hopper and I take St. Hildegard and the rest of the kittens to the back porch, the night insects calling to each other, and the stars overhead twinkling like a diamond quilt in the sky. The temperature is still around seventy, but the humidity has lifted.

We sit in the rockers, processing everything, but also just enjoying the peace. Neither of us is ready to say goodnight.

I hold up Hildy, staring into her eyes and she mews softly. To me, it sounds like, "Mamma."

My heart melts.

"Your birthday's tomorrow," Hopper says. "I haven't had a chance to get you anything."

His smiling face is all I need. "Just come to my party and I'll be happy."

Godfrey emerges from the shadows of the porch. He meows, but I hear, *I found her.*

"Found who?" I say and Hopper looks at me funny.

"Huh?"

"The cat." I point to Godfrey and see another shadow lurking beyond the steps. A white one that resembles Shade, but this one is flesh and bone. "I understand him like I do a human."

The porchlight barely illuminates us, but I can hear the incredulousness in Hopper's voice. "You're kidding."

I figure if he's accepted all the other weird stuff about me, he probably won't freak out over this. "Nope. Call me Dr. Doolittle. I sometimes hear animals talk." To the cat I say, "Who did you find, Godfrey?"

He lopes up the steps and sits at my feet. *Don't be scared,* he says to the other feline. *Fear is illogical.*

The figure moves to join him, her white fur glowing in the moonlight. Her eyes look like they are as well when she raises her head to me.

A meow. *Babies?*

"You're the mom?" My heart fills with gratitude to our annoying, self-important shop cat. "Nice to meet you. We've taken good care of them for you."

I lead her to the box, setting Hildy down inside. Mamma cat nuzzles her, then the others, waking the sleeping kittens.

"Wow," Hopper says, watching. "That's a really good thing."

I stroke Godfrey as the reunion continues. Mamma cat crawls in with them, gently shifting her little ones so she can lie down. The kittens begin to nurse as natural as can be.

Hopper takes my hand and we smile at each other.

Name's Snow, Godfrey tells me. *Her owners up and moved, left her and the kittens behind. She went to hunt for food, and when she came back, the babies were gone. She doesn't know who brought them to us.*

I relay what the cat has said to Hopper, but he doesn't seem surprised. "You can stay here," I tell Snow. "You and your babies are safe now."

She thanks me, Hopper kisses me, and for the first time in several days, I feel happy.

24

My birthday dawns clear and bright, I'm up early to watch the sunrise. Summer Solstice...the best day of the year.

I take a dip in the hot spring, Cinders keeping me company. Snow is taking good care of the kittens and I fed her before I left the cabin. She's underweight and I plan to fatten her up as quickly as possible.

After my dip in the rejuvenating waters, I find my sisters waiting at my place. Spring has baked my favorite cake, blueberry with powdered sugar icing, and Autumn has decorated the three tiers with tiny fairy figurines and real flowers.

Brightly colored candles are inserted around the top layer and Winter asks what my wish is. My sisters have that look in their eyes, telling me they already know.

I hold my breath, close my eyes, and imagine Hopper and I married with a couple kids. The Touch and my clair-voyance are gifts, not curses, and I'm trying to view them that way. If I'm lucky enough to have children, and they're born with either of my skills, I'll be able to teach them how to use them to help others.

After we eat and drink raspberry tea from Spring's stash, I hug my sisters and send them off. There's nothing better than cake for breakfast, especially with the three of them.

My birthday grants me a day off from the shop, and after I spend time with the kittens and Snow, I gather my tools for rock hunting.

The cave mouth is twenty yards from the main hot springs, and I'm hoping to find a special crystal to mark my day. Usually, I don't go alone, but my sisters don't enjoy the hunt as much as I do, and they all have plenty to do for the party tonight.

The sun is warm on my skin and I'm sure I'll end up with a few extra freckles. I have my hat with the headlamp, and I'm thinking about what I'll wear to the party as I climb the rocky slope past the bubbling springs and cabin ruins, making it to the cave entrance.

"Good morning, birthday girl."

I look up to find Hopper waiting beside the entrance. He's wearing good, sturdy boots, khaki pants, and a vest over a Rolling Stones t-shirt. The hat on his head echoes Indiana Jones, and he has a pick and a shovel in hand, a bucket at his feet, and a flashlight in his vest pocket.

I smile. "What are you doing here?"

"Before Winter puts me to work on building that wagon, I thought I'd do a little gold mining with my favorite witch."

"Hate to disappoint you but I haven't located that vein yet. Mostly, I find quartz, amethyst, and a few other stones."

"I'll make you a deal, if you find something you want turned into a ring, I'll make it for you."

"You're on."

The cave is cool and quiet, echoing our footsteps and

voices back to us as I lead him toward an area littered with rose quartz. I love the world of crystals. It fascinates me, and I babble like the springs outside about my favorite stones.

"I'm probably boring you to death," I say, as he uses the pickaxe to loosen a chunk of the cave wall.

"You are anything but boring." Carefully, as though he's handling a baby, he peels the piece loose and turns it so I can see a beautiful carpet of quartz. I shine the flashlight across them and am amazed at their clarity and the faint pink color emanating from them.

They barely need cleaning. Since Spring has my rose quartz necklace, I'm already imagining a new one.

We work at this section for a half hour, removing several large chunks of deeper pink. These will bring a nice price at the shop.

I take Hopper to one of my favorite spots deeper inside the cave, several feet lower than the entrance. Illumination filters down from a natural skylight onto water pooling in a circle. The air smells cleaner here, sharper.

The dappled sunlight has a rainbow effect on the surface and we stand for several seconds in silence, watching the ripples of color.

"It's beautiful," Hopper says. "I see why you like it here."

I lean into his arm, enjoying the feel of his solidness. "Thank you for coming."

"Summer?"

"Yes?"

"I want to tell you my secrets."

Oh boy. I wasn't expecting that. "You don't have to."

"You were brave enough to share yours with me, so here goes." He turns toward me and I see the soft light from the pool reflecting in his eyes. "Promise you won't laugh."

Double on the *oh boy*. "I promise."

"I love to cook,"—he takes a deep sigh—"but I suck at it."

I try not to laugh. "*That's* your secret?"

"I'm serious. It's really, *really* bad. I can't even make toast."

"Okay." I can't hold back the laugh. "So that's the reason you come to Conjure for breakfast every morning... Spring's bakery goods."

"Nah, because of you, but those are a bonus."

"Good to know."

Another serious, heavy sigh. "Also...I have a lot of money."

I already know this but play dumb. "And why is that a secret?"

"I'm afraid people will only like me for it, so I keep it on the down low. I made it from selling my grandparents healthy collection of art work when they passed ten years ago. It's one of the things that got me started in antiques."

"That's awesome."

"You already knew that didn't you?"

I try to stay serious and keep the grin off my face. "Not about the collection."

He rolls his eyes. "I can hear animals, too."

What? I simply stare at him for a long moment, brow shooting up. Are the acoustics in here messing with my hearing? "I'm sorry. What?"

"When I was in Special Forces in Iraq, I sustained a head injury. Lost my hearing for a while in both ears. When it began to come back, I could hear and understand certain animals."

My mouth falls open. "So, like Godfrey and the kittens?"

He nods. "You probably don't want to know what Godfrey says behind your back."

I'll kill that cat yet. "And you didn't tell me this sooner because...?"

A grin is his only answer. "There's one more secret."

"I'm not sure I can handle anything else."

He gently takes my hands, holding them by the fingers only. "I've been head over heels in love with you since the day I met you."

I don't know what to say. "We met three years ago—"

"—when you came into my shop looking for a nineteen-fifties pie bird for your mother's birthday," he finishes for me. "Yep, I've been pining over you that long."

My knees feel weak. I throw my arms around his neck. "I love you, Hopper Caldwell."

He buries his face in my hair, holding me close. "I love you, too, Summer Whitethorne."

Cinders flies in, squawking. The bird sips from the pool and stares at me. *You two done yet?*

Romantic moment over. "You're as bad as Godfrey sometimes," I reprimand the phoenix.

Hopper laughs and looks at the cave walls, glistening as if they're wet. "Do you get information from the crystals when you touch them?"

"Yes, but it's different from the kind of messages I get from people."

"How?"

I go over and touch the closest cave wall and feel the vibrations. I close my eyes, and in my mind's eye, I see color, hear a musical frequency that normal people might not register. It's much like a harmony, a symphony.

Rocks contain great wisdom, and their healing powers have been used throughout time by all cultures. "The Touch allows me to understand their frequencies. I know how certain crystals can help people feel better. I only wish more believed in them."

The next area I take Hopper to is a bounty for uncovering rubies and sapphires. I show him the area I've been working on for a while to find some for the shop. "Did you know rubies and sapphires are the same composition? They're both corundum,"

"Why do they come in different colors?"

"Impurities. Chromium creates red. Iron and titanium create blue."

He begins to dig, handing chunks to me. Our buckets full.

"Most of what I see coming into the shop is lab created," he says, admiring the chunk I'm cleaning. "I love when I find a genuine ruby or sapphire in vintage jewelry."

Returning to the hot spring, we clean the rest. Cinders suns himself on a nearby boulder.

I find a ruby that's gem quality. "Look." I hand it to Hopper. "I'd like a ring from this."

He holds it up to the sunlight and nods. "Perfect choice."

He follows me to my cabin where he checks on the kittens and strokes Snow's fur. She purrs and rubs her head against him. He then kisses me and leaves, telling me he'll see me later.

After I clean up and make lunch, I share it with the mother cat. She seems to want my attention even after I feed her, and I follow her to the box with the kittens, who are noisily meowing. As we get closer, I realize I can understand some of their excitement.

Snow and I both look inside, and I chuckle to myself. "Well, I'll be darned. Look at that, Momma."

Both Mozart and St. Hildy have their eyes open. Chopin

has managed to get one, and the three kittens are excitedly going on and on to the others about what they see.

Later that afternoon, I walk to the gazebo where a wagon has suddenly sprung out of air, thanks to Hopper and Hale's carpentry skills. I compliment them on it, and sneak a kiss from Hopper as he strings fairy lights on it.

Inside, Spring is making all kinds of treats for the party, while Autumn runs the shop.

Around three, Dad shows up, and he and I sit on the back porch, watching Hopper, Hale, and Storm transform the backyard into a midnight summer's dream. Twinkle lights are everywhere, along with lanterns on the trees, swaths of fabric and lots of flowers and garlands.

Autumn closes at five and Spring hustles me to my cabin to get ready. I pull out a long, tiered skirt, sparkling tank top, and a purple blouse with bell sleeves. Spring braids my hair and fixes a crystal headband around it. I add big hoop earrings and numerous rings.

We do each other's makeup as we listen to my favorite playlist of lighthearted music, and add a couple henna tattoos to our arms. We layer on scarves and laugh as we dance before we leave.

Friends bring gifts and their significant others. A couple clients stop by to wish me well and enjoy the pastries. Winter emerges from her cabin, dressed as a fortune teller, and we set up a table for her. Within minutes, she has a long line of customers.

Hale stokes a small bonfire and we pipe music outside from the shop. I show the group how to do a Celtic summer dance around the fire. Hopper is by my side through it, completely uncoordinated and trying not to fall over his own feet. A couple times, he nearly takes me down with him. I find his willingness to try extremely sexy.

By the time we're done, we're all laughing so hard we collapse. I lay there, looking at the stars and feeling lucky.

Autumn insists we do pictures using the wagon as a back drop. Clouds are moving in and a light rain puts a damper on our outdoor festivities. We move everything but the wagon inside.

Winter's friend, Avalon Fantome, from Atlanta, joins us. She's visiting relatives in town. She sees ghosts like Winter, but she's "in the closet," and doesn't want the general public to know. As an event planner, she might find her biz belly up if word gets out. Plus, her mom is mayor. Winter has so few friends that I'm happy Ava came, although it gives my sister a reason to shut down the popular fortune telling table.

My eldest sister may not have many good buddies, but she always says, "One best friend is all you need. I have four." I love thinking I'm one of them, but I know she sometimes feels more alone than she lets on, especially without Mom.

Autumn, on the other hand, has tons, and even a few guys who use the party as a reason to stop by and see her. She laughs a lot and sends them all on their way after a bit. Her heart belongs to one guy—her childhood sweetheart— the one man she believes she can't have, since he left Raven Falls several years ago after his brother died. It broke her heart.

Hopper bemoans the fact he didn't get his fortune told, but rounds up the rest of us for a game of charades with movie titles. Storm gets *The Wizard of Oz* to act out, Hale does *Up*! Spring gets *Jaws*. When it's his turn, Hopper reads the movie title on the paper and says, "Oh, this'll be too easy."

At that, he lays down, eyes staring vacantly up at the ceiling.

By the goddess. It's my vision of him on the floor at his shop all over again.

Only, he's not lying on *his*, but *mine*.

Relief bubbles up inside me so fast, it feels like I've downed a bottle of champagne and its fizzing right up my throat.

Winter shouts, "Dead man."

Autumn glances at me, sees the expression on my face and smiles.

Hopper jumps to his feet, snapping his fingers to let Winter know she's correct. Then he starts an exaggerated walk across the floor.

"Dead Man Walking," Dad says.

Hopper points to him and then to his nose. "Told you it was too easy."

I'm so in love with him I can't hold back the absolute relief that rushes over me. I hurry from the main room, fly through the kitchen, and out the back door to the porch.

Rain falls softly. Godfrey and Snow are sitting on the top step and both turn to look at me as I grab hold of the railing and laugh hysterically.

All that worry, all that fear. I wasn't seeing Hopper dead from a run-in with black magick. I was seeing the future and a silly party game.

Behind me, the screen door squeaks as Hopper joins me. "Hey, are you okay?"

"Perfect," I say. "Everything is perfect."

"I'll have your ring done by Monday." He draws me to him and kisses my cheek. "How about we go to dinner before I give it to you?"

I press my palms against his cheeks ready to answer, and the Touch kicks in, right through my lace gloves.

It's my original vision—Hopper, two kids, all of them

smiling and laughing. He's pushing one on a swing and looking back at a woman, saying something.

But this time, my vision pans out like a movie camera. I'm the woman. I see myself, wearing a ring—a beautiful ruby set in silver, a tiny dragon holding the stone in place.

My phoenix pendant heats on my collarbone. I see beautiful architecture in the distance. Two women walking by are chatting...

In French.

I'm in Paris. With Hopper. And two beautiful children.

The little girl runs up to me. "Mommy, Mommy, will you push me, too?"

I lift her into my arms, burying my nose in her neck. "*Bien sur.*"

She fingers my necklace. "It's glowing, Mommy."

"Just like my heart," I tell her.

In the next moment, Hopper is beside me, the boy in his arms. The kids look almost identical. Twins.

"Starting to rain," Hopper says. "Let's come back tomorrow."

He leans forward and kisses me softly.

The touch of his lips in that future timeframe snaps me back to the present.

I'm looking into his beautiful gray eyes, his brows drawn down. He's holding me close. "Another vision?"

I smile past my happy tears. "Yes," I say. I'm going to marry this man and have his children. We're going to Paris someday. "And this one is the best of all."

Keep reading for recipes, crafts, and a sneak peek at Of Spells and Stars, book 3 in the Sisters of Raven Falls Cozy Mystery series!!

ABOUT THE AUTHOR

Nyx Halliwell is a writer from the South who grew up on TV shows like Buffy the Vampire Slayer and Charmed. She loves writing magical stories as much as she loves baking and crafting. She believes cats really can talk, but don't tell her three rescue puppies that.

She enjoys binge-watching mystery shows with her hubby and reading all types of stories involving magic and animals.

Connect with Nyx today and see pictures of her pets, be the first to know about new books and sales, and find out when Godfrey, the talking cat, has a new blog post! Receive a FREE copy of the Whitethorne Book of Spells and Recipes by signing up for her newsletter http://eepurl.com/gwKHB9

DEAR READER

I hope you enjoyed this story! If you did, and would be so kind, would you leave a review on Goodreads and your favorite book retailer? I would REALLY appreciate it!

A review lets hundreds, if not thousands, of potential readers know what you enjoyed about the book, and helps them make wise buying choices. They might love it too, and try it out based on YOUR review! It's the best word-of-mouth around.

The review doesn't have to be anything long! Pretend you're telling a friend about the story. Pick out one or more characters, scenes, or dialogue that made you smile, laugh, or warmed your heart, and tell them about it. Just a few sentences is perfect!

And if you're interested in crystals, energy healing, astrology, and/or past lives, please visit https://crystalswithmisty.com/ or https://www.youtube.com/channel/UCZ5j1jwEmwr4L5GtXyM7lIA to find out more about how these all-natural, fun services can help you live a calmer, healthier life!

Blessed be,
Nyx 🖤

SIMPLE BLUEBERRY COFFEE CAKE RECIPE

Ingredients

- ½ cup butter, softened
- ¾ cup sugar
- 1 egg, room temperature
- 1 tsp. vanilla
- 2 cups flour
- 2 tsp. baking powder
- 1 tsp. salt
- 2 cups fresh blueberries
- ½ cup buttermilk
- 1 Tbsp. sugar, for sprinkling on top

Instructions

1. Preheat the oven to 350°F. Cream butter and sugar until light and fluffy.
2. Add the egg and vanilla and beat until combined.
3. Toss the blueberries with ¼ cup of flour.

4. In a separate bowl, whisk together the remaining flour, baking powder and salt.
5. Add the flour mixture to the batter a little at a time, alternating with the buttermilk. Fold in the blueberries.
6. Grease a 9-inch square baking pan with non-stick spray. Spread batter into pan. Sprinkle batter with remaining tablespoon of sugar. Bake for 35-45 minutes. Check with a toothpick for doneness. Let cool at least 15 minutes before serving.

Lavender Lemonade Recipe

Ingredients
   1 cup honey
   2 cups boiling water
   1 Tbsp. dried, organic culinary lavender (or 1/4 cup fresh lavender blossoms, crushed)
   1 cup fresh lemon juice (fresh squeezed, organic)
   2 cups cold water
   2-3 sprigs dried, organic culinary lavender (for garnish)

Directions:

Place the dried lavender in a pitcher; pour the boiling water over it; cover with plastic wrap and allow to steep 10 minutes; strain and discard the lavender and return the water to the pitcher. Add the honey and stir until dissolved. Add the lemon juice and cold water. Refrigerate until serving and garnish if desired.

Fairy party ideas:

Check thrift stores for fancy tea cups and saucers. Don't be afraid to mix and match, no set needs to be perfect.

Add small white lights to everything.

Use lots of small pots of flowers around sitting areas and on table, hang swags of greenery (decorated with lights) over doorways or fireplaces, and wrap colorful ribbons or scarves around everything.

Have temporary fairy tattoos available for guests.

Make a selection of miniature teacakes, muffins, fruit kabobs, etc. Add sprinkles and colored sugar (fairy dust) to any frosting you use.

Serve lavender or pink lemonade and label it Fairy Juice.

Print out a *What Is Your Fairy Name* sheet from Pinterest and let your guests become truly magickal!

Hold a fairy scavenger hunt, searching for things in nature, such as pinecones, flowers, leaves, twigs, moss, etc. You can also hide tiny bells and trinkets for guests to find just for fun.

If you're crafty, fill tiny bottles with glitter and make Fairy Dust necklaces for each of your guests to take home.

THE AMAZING HEALING ENERGIES OF CRYSTALS!

Rose Quartz

Unconditional love ~ Compassion ~ Gratitude

Aids in self-love, self-forgiveness

Attracts romance

Place over heart; wear as jewelry; carry in pockets or purse. Place several stones in bowls inside house or on desk. Works well with other stones.

Black Tourmaline

Protection ~ Grounding

Stops all negativity, including EMF and geopathic

Wear as jewelry; place in four corners of house, room, or office to stop others' negativity from entering. Works well with selenite, rose quartz, and other high vibration stones.

Selenite

Cleansing ~ Protection ~ Healing

Cleans energy on all levels

Shields energy from outside forces

Enhances psychic abilities

Promotes sleep and peace

Place under pillow or bed; place in any room, windows, corners, on desk, etc. If feeling sick, place on appropriate body part.

Commonly asked questions:

What is Reiki? Reiki is an energy healing modality that clears and balances your chakras and aura with pure Source (Universal Consciousness, God, whatever you prefer to call it) energy. It is unconditional love and healing that aids you in releasing stress, raising your body's own healing frequency, and being at peace with your life.

What is Crystal Healing? Crystal healing uses the natural vibrational frequency of the stones to affect positive, healing energy flow in the body. Like Reiki, it raises your natural vibration, clearing out toxins and that which no longer serves you so healthy energy can come in.

If you'd like to learn more about crystals, schedule a healing session, or contact a loved one who's passed over, please visit: www.crystalswithmisty.com

SNEAK PEEK AT STARS AND SPELLS!

Dive into the next magical story, Spells and Stars, Sister Witches of Raven Falls, Book 3, and find out if star-crossed lovers can create an enchanting new life together as they uncover the truth about a very human threat.

Chapter 1

Autumn. My favorite season and the one I'm named after. This morning, I feel the tug of the Pacific Northwest weather, the turning of the wheel of life, even before I open my front door.

Something big is happening today. Even my cards agree. The Ace of Pentacles fell out of my tarot deck as I shuffled this morning, alerting me to new beginnings and earth energy working together to bring me something tangible.

Crisp fall air fills my nose as I find Godfrey and Snow perched on the welcome mat. Both cats look up at the same time, as if their heads are on a string, and Godfrey meows loudly.

Cats. I have a doggie door at the back entrance, but they refuse to use it. Godfrey believes it's beneath him, and he's trained his new love interest to act the same.

The two walk by me, one on each side. They curl up at the fireplace, Snow nestling in among her kittens and licking Vivaldi's head before she settles on Sirius's large dog bed. Sirius is my familiar, a beautiful large Irish wolfhound that Snow's kittens adore.

The kittens have grown considerably since my sister, Summer, found them in a box left on the front porch of our metaphysical shop this past June. Vivaldi, along with the others, greets her mother warmly and rubs her face with her own.

As I look out across the yard, I inhale deeply, enjoying the beautiful sunlight glistening off an abundance of yellow, orange, and red leaves. Winter's cabin and the Whitethorne woods are on my right. Summer and Spring's cabins, several gardens, and Spring's greenhouse, branch off on the left. Gourds and pumpkins are scattered amongst the now dormant gardens, Mother Nature getting ready for a deep sleep.

Sirius is finishing his breakfast, and is ready for his walk, by the time I've slipped on my running shoes. I'm wearing bright orange yoga pants featuring pumpkins and a matching puffy vest over a black long-sleeve shirt. I've swept my red hair into a ponytail and put in my skeleton earrings to complete my look. Sirius wears a black collar with moons and stars on it, his metal tag a bright yellow, matching the color of his wise old eyes.

My familiar and I leave the cats by the fireplace to nap in its warmth, and head out for our daily jaunt.

Yellow and purple mums are in full bloom along the stone path to Conjure. The last traces of fog slips off amongst the pines and redwoods, and the sun continues to rise. The smell of baking apples and pumpkin bread mixes with the scent of the pine trees, telling me Spring is hard at work in the kitchen for the fall festival and Samhain celebration.

Sirius trots on and off the path, sniffing and marking his territory here and there. I feel more alive at this time of year than any other, and the dog seems to share that.

Spring's familiar, Hoax, is on the back porch as we climb the steps. "May there be guineafowl crying at your child's birth," the mockingbird yells at me.

Whatever that means. Sirius growls at him in warning, but I just roll my eyes. The bird is cursed and can't fly, and he slings Irish and Gaelic curses at everyone—his way of mocking us. Some days, I wonder how he's managed to live this long among a group of witches.

I leave Sirius on the back porch with Hoax, and head inside to find Spring and her friend, Storm, baking apple fritters, donuts, and other specialty treats for the case out front. I greet my sister, whose pale cheeks are flushed from the heat of the stove, with a kiss on the cheek. Snagging a cup from the cabinet, I fill it with warm apple cider from a giant soup pot on the stove.

Storm, a gypsy at heart, pulls out the latest round of miniature apple cider donuts from the oven. She's pinned her long hair up on top of her head and wears a black flowing skirt, purple top, and a candy corn necklace. Her dark hair and eyes contrast Spring's blond hair and blue eyes, but the two move with a rhythm suggesting they are old friends reunited in this lifetime. Spring sprinkles cinnamon sugar on top of the donuts and then puts them on a cooling rack.

I drop a cinnamon stick into the apple cider and take several sips, enjoying the scent and warmth as it goes down my throat. "How many have you made?" I ask, looking around. Every inch of counterspace is covered with some form of baked goods. I lick my lips anticipating what I'm sneaking from the plethora for breakfast.

"We've completed three dozen donuts," my sister says, continuing to work even as she speaks. Her dangling black cat earrings swing as she moves. She's wearing my favorite Halloween apron and she accented her outfit with an orange and black headband. "I have five dozen more, three pies, and two dozen pumpkin muffins on order."

Along with her lotions, potions, and herbs, her bakery goods are in high demand. She's probably been here in the kitchen since well before sunrise. "When I get back from my run, I'll open up the shop so you two can keep working. My clients don't start until ten. That will give you time to get your orders completed."

As she hustles past me, she gives me a quick squeeze. "Thank you." She points to a basket on the edge of the counter. "Will you drop that at Mama Nightingale's?"

"Of course." Snatching up the basket, I return to the porch, grab Sirius, and the two of us take off. As we pass the front parking lot, I see there are already customers lining up at the entrance, hoping to be one of the few to grab the apple cider donuts before they sell out.

Even with Storm's help, Spring has been running out of all the fall pastries by the end of each day. I expect the holidays will be the same.

The shop is also short of space to keep up with demand for other products, especially Summer's crystal jewelry, and our selection of buddhas and goddess statues. I've been considering expanding our storefront on the north side to give us more room. We could use the retail space for products and I could use a larger treatment room.

I don't do many energy healing sessions—that's Summer's area of expertise—but I'm seeing more clients than ever for tarot readings, birth chart readings, and relationship advice. They often come in pairs or groups and it's challenging to fit everyone around my table.

Summer has seen an increase in her energy healing sessions as well, and I know she could use more space in her room for all her crystals and other supplies. Sometimes, she has couples or best friends who want to have a treatment together, but she only can fit one table in there. She recently had a request to do an entire bridal party, giving them all a burst of positive energy to get them through the wedding, but it's impossible to squeeze that many people into the tiny room she uses now, so she was forced to do the group session at the bride's house.

Plus, Spring needs a bigger kitchen. Then we could hire Storm full time.

Expansion—this energy falls under the planet Jupiter. I ask for that planet's guidance and assistance as I contemplate my plans.

The sounds of birds and squirrels getting ready for hibernation reach my ears. Sirius and I turn north, walking along the highway on our favorite bike trail. I drink in the sight of the turning leaves, the reassuring smell of wood fires lingering in the air.

Various evergreens provide a canopy over the trail, a tapestry of sunshine falling at our feet. I have to watch for acorns and pinecones as I start a jog to keep up with Sirius. I take him off leash so he can run along the path in and out of the woods, sniffing and barking at the squirrels.

We pass the rear of Momma Nightingale's convenience store, and it looks like she's busy this early as well. Several people are getting gas, others coming and going from the store with various prepackaged items, newspapers, and lottery tickets. Mama herself opens the back door to throw out trash and says good morning to me. I lift the basket, whistle at Sirius to come, and after a logging truck passes, we cross the highway to deliver the breakfast goods for her new fresh bakery case.

"You tell your sister I'm needin' more," she says, flipping back the red-checkered towel to eye the contents. "I'm selling out of these goodies every morning before I can say Happy Halloween."

I smile at the shorter woman, the sun on her dark skin highlighting its smooth surface. I wonder how old our neighbor is—much older than she appears I suspect. "She's having trouble keeping up with the demand at our place too, but I'll put in your request."

One of Mama's eyes narrows at me. "She puttin' some kind of spell of them, making them so popular?"

I wink at her. "Good food is a magick in itself, isn't it?"

She laughs good-naturedly and pats Sirius on the head. "I'm lookin' forward to your trick-or-treat open house Saturday night. Need me some new tarot cards."

"They'll be on sale."

She nods, looking off toward the woods. "Your momma would be proud of what you gals accomplished in the past year, growing Conjure the way you have."

My heart does a hard thud in my ribcage at the thought of Mom. "We're having a small get-together after the open house to honor her if you'd like to attend."

Another nod, this time her gaze finding mine. "I'd be honored."

With a wave goodbye, Sirius and I head back to the path.

My heart does another thud, this one more like a soft echo, as we draw close to Harrington Farms. The twenty-five acre family-owned and operated place grows vegetables for sale in the summer, pumpkins and gourds in autumn, and Christmas trees for the holidays.

There's a small wooden stand behind the front gate, pumpkins in various sizes spreading out from each side. Potted mums form a backdrop. Inside the stand are jars of homemade jams and jellies, and some of Spring's honey, along with other craft items Mrs. Harrington makes and sells.

I'm surprised to see the gate is closed. No one is in the stand. Usually when Sirius and I go by, Mr. or Mrs. Harrington, or one of their helpers, is opening up.

The house seems quiet as well. There's no one out and about.

I feel an itch under my breastbone, but I ignore it, running on with Sirius. Perhaps they're getting a late start today, or having a business meeting inside.

We run past acres of ground, now going fallow for the winter. Mr. Harrington has already cleaned off most of the garden growth and vines, a few beds still filled with mums. Behind that are acres of Christmas trees, the next season bearing down on us even though Halloween is a couple days away.

My sisters and I celebrate the holiday as Samhain, and our customers who do the same are growing every year, demanding more and more items for the season. The Harringtons have seen a good amount of growth in the past few years as well. Many folks have come full circle, wanting the experience of hunting for pumpkins, purchasing locally grown mums and gourds, and preferring handmade gift items rather than the mass produced and marketed items from stores.

Sirius and I spend a little time in the national park, soaking up sun and passing other walkers, joggers, and bike riders. Everyone in these parts speaks and offers a kind word, and I offer gratitude to Mother Nature for giving us this beautiful place to live in.

I gather a few maple leaves from the path—as big as my hand and strikingly yellow and orange—before we turn around and head home. I plan to press them in our Whitethorne Book of Spells I keep to infuse the pages with the precious fall energy.

Several cars pass us on the highway as we walk the bike path back toward the Harrington Farm. I'm thinking about the clients I have later today—two tarot readings, and a past life birth chart analysis. I always enjoy those a great deal.

I'm thinking about that and the possible expansion of our shop next year, when a black truck roars past me and wheels in at the Harrington's drive.

A man gets out dressed in a perfectly pressed white military uniform. I stop in my tracks and my breath catches in my lungs.

I'd know that build, that beautiful head of hair, that face, anywhere.

He goes to the gate to unlock it.

I blink several times, unable to believe my eyes. This Air Force officer is broader and more muscled under that impressive uniform than I man I knew five years ago.

But my heart has no doubt, its solid thudthudthud inside my chest an absolute checkmark.

Quinn.

My soul mate.

Sirius stops beside me, his lanky body pressing into my leg as he picks up on my sudden mix of emotions—surprise, worry...

Love.

A bottomless well of unrequited love.

For half a second, I try to talk myself out of the idea that it truly is Quinn Harrington. He's swung the gate open so he can drive up the lane leading to the house.

His buzzcut hair is so dark, it seems to absorb the morning sunlight. When he looks up, his eyes meet mine, and there's no denying it.

I sense him catch his breath.

This is the man who left me five years ago.

The man whose chart I've read a hundred times.

Unlike the dozens of couples decorating the wall in my office, ours isn't a fairy tale ending. We're soul mates, yes, but not all soul mates end up together.

My love life is jinxed. In this lifetime, Quinn and I are destined to only be star-crossed lovers.

Doesn't mean I've stopped caring for him. Dreaming about him. Wishing on the stars that he'd back down to earth to be with me.

Wish granted.

Or is it?

My pulse beats so fast I feel like I might have a panic attack. I feel his heartbeat too—clairsentience is one of my gifts. It's as if the two of us are frozen in time.

How is it possible that he's back and I didn't know it?

The eclipse! The Ace of Pentacles warned me, and we're between a solar and lunar eclipse, the lunar one coming on Samhain. Eclipses reveal secrets and brings surprises—and not always good ones.

Beside me, Sirius whines. I pet the dog's head, reassuring him. I lift the other hand in hello to Quinn, and the action seems to snap him out of his surprise. Nothing changes in his face, and he gets into his truck and pulls it through the gate as if he doesn't know me.

My heart drops like a fifty pound pumpkin into my stomach.

Grab your copy today! *Of Stars and Spells*

BOOKS BY NYX HALLIWELL

Sister Witches Of Raven Falls Mystery Series

Of Potions and Portents
Of Curses and Charms
Of Stars and Spells
Of Spirits and Superstition

Confessions of a Closet Medium Cozy Mystery Series
(Coming 2020)

Psychic Sisters Cozy Mystery Series
(Coming 2021)

CONNECT WITH NYX TODAY!

Website: nyxhalliwell.com
Facebook: https://www.facebook.com/NyxHalliwellAuthor/
Twitter: @HalliwellNyx
Instagram: https://www.instagram.com/nyxhalliwellauthor/
Email: nyxhalliwellauthor@gmail.com
Bookbub https://www.bookbub.com/profile/nyx-halliwell
Amazon amazon.com/author/nyxhalliwell

Sign up for Nyx's Cozy Clues Mystery Newsletter and be the FIRST to learn about new releases, sales, behind-the-scenes trivia about the book characters, pictures of Nyx's pets, and links to insightful and often hilarious *From the Cauldron With Godfrey blog*!

Made in United States
Orlando, FL
14 January 2023

28683278R00119